AS THE
CROW FLIES

ALSO BY DAMIEN BOYD

Head in the Sand

Kickback

DAMIEN BOYD

AS THE CROW FLIES

THOMAS & MERCER

Published by Thomas & Mercer, Seattle

www.apub.com

Amazon, the Amazon logo, and Thomas & Mercer are trademarks of Amazon.com, Inc., or its affiliates.

ISBN-13: 978-1477821039
ISBN-10: 1477821031

Cover concept by Littera Designs
Cover created by bürosüd° München, www.buerosued.de

Library of Congress Control Number: 2014947409

Printed in the United States of America

For Shelley

Prologue

As the Crow Flies; E7 6c 130 ft; A direct finish to the classic Crow (E3 5c/6a***). From Crow pitch 3 ignore the traverse left and continue direct to a hanging stance under the left hand end of the small overhang. Pegs. Continue direct over the left hand of the small overhang via a shallow chimney to enter the shallow crack above. Follow the crack to its finish. RP2 (last gear). Continue direct up the exposed and bulging wall above (crux) to finish in the shallow groove. Exit. Very exposed and strenuous.

He had been working on it for two years on and off. The restrictions in the gorge didn't help, limiting climbing on the south side to the winter months, but he knew he was getting close. He had managed each of the moves individually, several sections in sequence, and was now working on stringing those sequences together.

It made for a relaxing evening after work, on the rare occasions he was working and for the few weeks before the clocks went back. Then it would become weekends only. Abseil in to the peg belay and climb out. Perfectly safe but the tourists loved it. He wondered how many photographs had been taken of him over the years.

Today was no different. The early autumn sun was catching the top of High Rock as he abseiled in to the hanging stance. He fed the rope through the belay plate with his right hand and held the Petzl Shunt open in his left. Just below the small overhang he clipped into the pegs and then hung his rucksack on the end of the rope to keep it taut. He removed the belay plate and was now free to climb out. The Shunt would move freely up the rope with him but lock to catch him when he fell.

He had mastered the first sequence some time ago. He made short work of the small overhang and then sat back on the rope for a rest at the base of the shallow crack above. His forearms were screaming at him. He was fit but knew he would need to be fitter when the time came for the first ascent.

The shallow crack would be particularly strenuous because he would be using one hand to fix what meagre protection was available. A Friend 2 low down in the flared crack and an RP2 higher up, the last before the crux twenty feet above. He was determined that this would be a clean first ascent. The route offered a long fall onto precious little gear but there would be nothing to hit on the way down and no chance of reaching the ground. That was the advantage of starting the route three hundred feet up.

The exit from the crack to become established on the wall above was the key to unlocking the next sequence. He sat on the rope for several minutes to rest and worked through the moves in his mind. In the still evening air he could hear shouts from below and the clicking of cameras. Better put on a good show for the holidaymakers.

It was right at the limit of his reach to make the first handhold on the wall from the top of the crack. The footholds were thin at best. He reached out and up with his right hand and made a lunge for the handhold above just as his feet slipped. Fuck it. The screams from below told him that it must have looked spectacular from the ground as he swung out from the rock face on the end of the rope, his arms and legs flailing in thin air.

On the second attempt he managed to get his left foot a fraction higher. This was the key. Another sequence unlocked. Today was proving to be productive.

The crux offered technically the hardest climbing, he thought grade 6c, but he had rehearsed it many times. The wall bulged making it gently overhanging for the most part and exceptionally strenuous. He had yet to complete it in one go but was getting closer with each attempt.

He reached into the bag on the back of his harness for fresh chalk and took several deep breaths. Two testing moves and then a rest of sorts on the only decent holds on the wall. A good start. More chalk and more deep breaths. Now for the crux.

It took just a moment to register that the rope in front of him had gone slack. He was taking his own weight on the rock but the rope should still not be slack. It took another moment to realise that the rope was getting slacker.

He looked up to see the rope above, his lifeline, falling towards him. Instinctively he braced himself. If the rope did not knock him off then the weight of it falling would pull him off. He could only close his eyes and wait.

He felt the rope hit his back as it fell past him. He felt the sudden weight of it pulling down on him, and then it stopped. The third alternative had not occurred to him. He had hung on.

He reached down gingerly with his left hand and released the bar on the Shunt to allow the rope to feed through. The weight of the rucksack should pull it through. It worked. The rope and rucksack fell to the ground.

He was now free of the trailing rope but had only one way out. Up. He had not completed the crux sequence in one go before but if he was going to do it, it had to be now.

He tried to move but couldn't. He was frozen. Movement up or down was no longer an option. Then he began to shake. It started in his left leg, almost imperceptibly at first, before it began to overtake him.

He had seen climbers shake themselves off the rock face before and now it was his turn. The shaking became more violent with the passing of each second. He was out of control. The realisation of what was about to happen hit home. Tears began to stream down his face.

He thought about his parents and his girlfriend. The end when it came would, at least, be quick.

Chapter One

Very few people had understood his decision to leave the Metropolitan Police and join the Avon and Somerset force, but Nick Dixon had never regretted it for a minute. Walking along the base of the cliffs at Brean Down on a gloriously sunny morning in early autumn, he was reminded more than ever that it had been the right decision. There was not a soul around, the tide was out and the wet sand glistened in the low morning sun.

Ambition and career had never been all that important to him and it had always been his intention to return home at the first opportunity. Career advancement in the police meant management and he wasn't having that either. Crime detection was what it was about for him. He had to concede that the quality of work was better in the Met but that had never really motivated him either. It was just a job. A job doing what he enjoyed and now in a place he loved. Definitely the right decision.

His girlfriend had certainly not understood, making it abundantly clear, shortly before she became his ex-girlfriend, that she had no intention of burying herself away in the back end of beyond.

His parents had not understood it either. It was always expected that he would go on to become the Metropolitan Police

Commissioner with a knighthood at the very least, and they never missed an opportunity to remind him how much his education had cost and the sacrifices that had been made along the way. They had left him in no doubt that his decision was an enormous disappointment to them.

Dixon had graduated from university with a degree in law and had gone on to qualify as a solicitor. Only then had he opted for a career in the police. Being a graduate, his promotion had been fast tracked to the rank of inspector, a fact that was openly resented by most of his colleagues. Much to the irritation of his superiors, he had then insisted on a switch to CID. He had spent five years based in Wimbledon before the transfer to the Avon and Somerset force came up.

He was not entirely convinced that his new colleagues in the Avon and Somerset force understood why he had transferred from the Met either. Various rumours were circulating, each with a different reason for what was universally believed to have been his removal in circumstances that needed to be hushed up. Dixon took the view that no one would believe the simple truth that he wanted to move, so he had given up trying to explain.

The move itself had been a bit of a rush. He had gone from a furnished flat in Wimbledon to an unfurnished cottage in Brent Knoll, both rentals, and, two months on, his only furniture consisted of a bed and a TV. He had also needed a car. For those living inside the M25 a car is an unnecessary expense, particularly when public transport is so readily available. The same cannot be said for life in rural Somerset. Dixon had opted for a blue long wheelbase Land Rover Defender that had clearly seen better days. He had also invested in the relevant Haynes manual and was determined to do all the work on it himself.

Dixon's most recent acquisition, if acquisition was the right word, was an eight month old white Staffordshire bull terrier he had called Monty. A cheerful soul, despite what he had been through; Monty had come from a rescue centre and had been found abandoned. Dixon felt sure that Monty had never been allowed to run off the lead before but he was certainly making up for it now. He was also getting the hang of chasing a tennis ball. Bringing it back could come later.

Dixon walked out as far as Boulder Cove and sat on a rock to take in the view. He noticed the chalk marks on the cliffs above. It was obviously still a popular spot with local climbers. He was aware that the tide was coming in now and knew from experience that it raced across the flats at a fast walking pace. No place for the unwary. He tucked Monty under his arm and scrambled up the steep path to the left of the Cove. When he reached the top he stopped to put Monty's lead on, remembering many years before finding a Staffordshire terrier dead at the foot of the cliffs. He had rung the owners to break the news. It had been chasing rabbits. He had broken worse news to many more people since.

He was standing on the gun emplacement near the Fort when his phone rang.

'Dixon.'

'Harding, Sir. Sorry to trouble you on a Sunday.'

'No problem, Dave. What's up?'

'We've had a John Fayter on the phone, several times, asking for you.'

'What does he want?'

'His son's been killed in a climbing accident at Cheddar Gorge. On Friday evening.'

It was a solid blow to the pit of Dixon's stomach.

'Jake?'

'Yes, Sir. Do you know him?'

'I do.'

'Mr Fayter's asking to see you. He says it's urgent. He lives at . . .'

'. . . Burnham-on-Sea. I know. Ring him back and tell him I'm on my way, will you?'

The walk back to his car took Dixon twenty minutes. What should have been an enjoyable walk in the sunshine became a sombre trip down memory lane. He had first met Jake Fayter when he left school. Dixon had arrived home determined to take up rock climbing. He had got a job manning the putting green at Burnham-on-Sea and this had paid for a pair of climbing boots, a harness, a rope, a few bits of gear and a chalk bag. Then he cycled to Brean Down to make a start. That he got home at all that evening had been down to Jake.

Jake recognised straight away that Dixon had no real idea what he was doing and offered to lead him up Pandora's Box, a very inviting VS 4c crack at the right hand end of Ocean Wall. In at the deep end for a novice but Dixon had made short work of it. It marked the start of a successful climbing partnership that lasted until shortly before Dixon left for London to join the Met.

It had quickly become apparent to Dixon that there are two types of climber: those who push their limits and those who push *the* limits. He accepted early on that he was going to have to be content with pushing his own limits but it was equally clear that Jake was determined to push *the* limits. Climbing trips to Wales, the Peak District and the Lakes had followed, pretty much every weekend, with Dixon spending most of his time holding Jake's rope. He was able to match Jake technically, perhaps, but he had never been able to match him on the lead. That ability to climb above the last piece of protection and take the consequences had always eluded him.

It came to an end for Dixon one afternoon at Stanage. It was a rare occasion for him to lead and he and Jake had been waiting their turn on Left Unconquerable, the classic E1 5b. Looking back on it, he was convinced it happened in slow motion but what he remembered most of all was the noise. A single runner in the horizontal crack. He had never understood that. The climber slipped, the runner pulled out and he had landed flat on his back right next to Dixon. A loud crack. The Air Ambulance had arrived within half an hour.

Three days later Dixon had left for London and had never climbed again. He had kept in touch with Jake for a while, and they had gone for a curry on the rare occasions when he was home, but even that had petered out over time. Jake had kept a blog enabling Dixon to keep up with his new routes. He had subscribed to email alerts too but it had not been updated for a while, so Dixon had felt sure that Jake was working on something big. They had often talked about the direct finish to Crow and he wondered whether that was what Jake had been working on. They had talked about dying too.

Dixon stood on the doorstep of the small double fronted bungalow in Braithwaite Place for what seemed like an age before he finally rang the doorbell. Nothing much appeared to have changed over the years. The roses either side of the garden path were still immaculate although the windows needed a touch of paint, perhaps. Dixon noticed two cars in the drive. A Honda Civic and a Subaru Impreza that he guessed belonged to Jake. He had always enjoyed a fast car.

John Fayter was a small man with thinning grey hair and a white moustache. He greeted Dixon with a firm handshake and as warm a smile as he could manage in the circumstances.

'Hello, Nick. Thank you for coming.'

'Hello, Mr Fayter.'

'Do call me John, please—we've known each other long enough by now, I think.'

'I will. How are you these days, if that's not a stupid question?'

The look on John Fayter's face told Dixon that it had been a stupid question.

'Bearing up. You remember Maureen?'

Maureen Fayter appeared in the hallway. She immediately threw her arms around Dixon and burst into tears. Dixon could feel her body heaving as she sobbed. She tried to speak but no words would come. Dixon put his arms around her and looked at John Fayter, who shrugged. Dixon remembered the stiff upper lip that comes with a life in the Royal Marines and thought that this was probably the first time that Maureen Fayter had been able to let her grief show.

'How about a cup of tea?' John moved towards the kitchen but Maureen waved him away and went through to the back of the bungalow. Dixon could still hear her sobbing as he and John Fayter moved into the sitting room.

'It's nice to see you again, John. I'm only sorry that it's in these circumstances.'

'It's something we always feared might happen but never really thought it would, if that makes any sense.'

'It does.'

Dixon thought that John Fayter was about to burst into tears. His eyes welled up and his lip trembled when he spoke.

'They're going to have to identify him from DNA, apparently. He fell over four hundred feet so there's not a lot left of him . . . I haven't told Maureen . . .' His voice tailed off.

Dixon took the initiative.

'Has the coroner been informed?'

'Yes. I've spoken to the coroner's officer and a PC Cole from Wells rang to say that he's been asked to investigate. He told me about the identification.'

'Is that Jake's car outside, the Subaru?'

'Yes, that's Jake's. I didn't know what else to do with it so I told them to bring it here. At least it's off road. The tax has expired. Silly arse.'

'Do we know what happened yet?'

'Not really. He fell from near the top of High Rock so he must have been working on the direct finish to Crow. That was his pet project. PC Cole said that there were some witnesses on the ground. Tourists. They'd been taking photos immediately before he fell. He was on his own, of course.'

'That means he must have abseiled in and been climbing out on a Shunt?'

'That's right. They've recovered his climbing gear, which is intact. PC Cole's theory is that the rope came undone.'

Maureen arrived with the tea on a tray. Cups and saucers and cake.

'You really didn't need to go to all that trouble on my account, Maureen.'

'It's no trouble, really.' She poured the tea. 'John has told you they think it was an accident?'

'I said that PC Cole thinks Jake's rope came undone. I mean, for Christ's sake, Nick, how many times have you ever known that happen?'

Dixon thought for a moment. 'It's not a mistake a climber makes twice.'

'No, it isn't. And it's not a mistake Jake would make . . . would have made.' John glanced across to Maureen, who pretended not to have noticed.

'We always used to use a reef knot with a half hitch either side. The more you pull on it, the tighter it gets. If he'd abseiled over High Rock then there is no way that knot could or should have come undone.'

'Exactly,' said John. 'Look, we don't know what happened, obviously, but we don't want it just written off as an accident without proper investigation. It needs looking at by someone who understands climbing and, preferably, someone who knew Jake as well.'

'All we are asking is that you keep an eye on the investigation,' said Maureen. 'Make sure that no stone is left unturned. Please. You owe it to Jake.'

'I do. I'll do what I can, of course.'

'How is your diabetes these days?' asked Maureen. 'Is it a problem in the police?'

'No, not at all. I'm not allowed to drive response cars but then I wouldn't do that anyway in CID. Apart from that, I just have to demonstrate that I've not had a hypo recently, and I've got it under control now so that's no problem either.'

'Good. I remember when you were diagnosed. It was quite sudden, wasn't it?'

'Yes.'

Dixon felt the need to change the subject.

'Where was Jake living?'

'He was renting a flat in The Grove behind the tennis club with his girlfriend, Sarah,' replied Maureen.

'Sarah? What happened to Ruth?'

'They split up about a year ago. Then he met Sarah and moved in with her. He still has his room here as well.'

'Do I know Sarah?'

'You may do. She used to work in the Clarence, apparently. I'm not sure what she does now,' replied John.

'Was he working?'

'Not officially. He did a bit of cash in hand work but spent most of his time climbing. He did the high work on the roller coaster at the leisure centre. Cash, of course. That sort of thing.'

'Ok. I'll speak to PC Cole tomorrow and see what I can find out. It may not be much at this stage but I'll let you know. Can you let me have the number of the coroner's officer you spoke to, John?'

John Fayter went out into the hall to fetch a pen and paper from the sideboard. Dixon could see that Maureen was struggling to keep her composure.

'I have to know what happened to him . . .' Her voice tailed off as she began to sob.

John came back into the room and sat next to Maureen. He put his arm around her.

Dixon wrote his mobile phone number on the bottom of the piece of paper John had handed to him. He tore it off and then handed it back.

'That's my mobile phone number. If anything comes up you think I need to know, please, just give me a ring.'

'So, what happens now?' asked John.

'PC Cole will take statements from all of the witnesses and I would expect him to get hold of any photographs taken by the tourists at the time as well.'

'Will we get to see them?'

'Not initially, Maureen. But you will at the inquest.'

'I feel much better knowing that you will be involved.'

'It'll have to be unofficially, and remember that I am relatively new around here too, which doesn't help.'

'I understand that, but remember, Nick, no stone unturned. Promise me.'

Dixon drove along Berrow Road and turned right into Allandale Road. He drove to the end and parked overlooking the sea. It was a familiar view across to Hinkley Point but he was staring into space.

Maureen Fayter had been quite right, of course. Dixon did owe Jake. Jake had saved him on more than one occasion but then Dixon had done the same for him. Such was the nature of a climbing partnership.

Dixon had to admit that the incident Maureen had been referring to was out of the ordinary. Jake had gone above and beyond the call of duty. It had been soon after Dixon had been diagnosed with diabetes and he had not got the hang of controlling his blood sugar levels. They had been on a trip to Pembroke and were in Huntsman's Leap. A favourite spot. Dixon had been leading Quiet Waters E3 6a when he had a hypo above the crux. His blood sugar levels dropped, his strength went and he fell off. Left helpless, he needed sugar immediately.

Without hesitation, Jake had tied him off at the bottom of the cliff and then climbed up alongside him, unroped, with a Mars bar in his chalk bag. They had laughed about it later in the pub at St Govan's. They marked it down as a solo ascent of Quiet Waters by Jake, against the clock too, but the consequences of failure would have meant death for both of them.

On another occasion, Dixon had been leading Poetry Pink E5 6a in the slate quarries at Llanberis. With the last bolt at twenty-five feet and the crux at fifty feet, a fall from the crux meant that he would have landed on the terrace where Jake was standing. Dixon had frozen and Jake had seen that his legs had started to shake. Jake had also noticed that the rope was looped around Dixon's right leg and realised that he would be flipped upside down when he fell, hitting the terrace head first.

When Dixon fell, Jake stepped back and jumped off the terrace to take up the slack rope. No hesitation. No shout. He just jumped. Dixon stopped, hanging upside down two feet above the terrace.

Dixon took a deep breath, put his seatbelt on and started the engine. He looked across at Monty sitting on the passenger seat with his tennis ball in his mouth. He switched off the engine, reached across and opened the passenger door. Monty didn't need a second invitation and Dixon needed some fresh air.

Chapter Two

Dixon had never been a huge fan of Monday mornings and today was no exception. It was to be his first appearance in court since joining the Avon and Somerset force, and experience told him that he could look forward to several hours of waiting around followed by the entry of a late guilty plea and an early lunch. He had been the arresting officer on a routine case of grievous bodily harm resolved with the assistance of CCTV and a confession. The only argument left was whether the assault amounted to grievous bodily harm or the lesser offence of unlawful wounding.

Dixon found his suit still packed at the bottom of a suitcase and, whilst slightly crumpled, it would have to do. He decided to call in at Bridgwater Police Station on his way to Taunton Crown Court and quickly realised his mistake when DCI Lewis spotted him.

DCI Lewis was Dixon's immediate superior and whilst they had not yet had occasion to fall out, it could not be said that they had exactly hit it off either. Lewis was a copper's copper. At least that was the cliché Dixon heard used many times to describe men like Lewis. He was certainly one of the lads, with the leather jacket and beer belly to show for it.

Dixon had taken over Operation Magpie a week earlier and Lewis was keen to know what progress he had made in the investigation. Magpie was a countywide investigation into an organised gang burgling empty properties and taking only documents to be used for identity theft. The gang appeared to be targeting properties where the owner had recently died; at least that was Dixon's theory. He had been cross-referencing the bereavement notices in the local papers with the burglaries and had come across a pattern of sorts. DCI Lewis appeared impressed.

'What's your next step?'

'I'm going to place a fake death notice in the paper and lie in wait for the buggers, Sir. Or rather, the property will be placed under surveillance, budgetary constraints permitting.'

'Sounds like a plan, let me know what you need. Incidentally, I can let you have DS Gorman now that he has put the Williams case to bed.'

'Williams case?'

'The girl who died from an ecstasy overdose in the loos at Rococo's. Anyway, you had better be off to court.'

Gorman was certainly methodical and would be useful after the arrests were made but Dixon doubted that he would be much help if a surveillance operation turned nasty. Gorman made sure everyone knew that he had played prop forward for the Somerset Police 1st XV, but Dixon reckoned that was a good few years ago. Time and too much beer had definitely not been kind to him since then. At least he didn't wear a leather jacket.

CID occupied the top floor of the purpose built Bridgwater Police Station. One of the advantages of his rank was that it afforded Dixon his own office, although cubicle was a more accurate description and he had to share it with another DI, Janice Courtenay.

'You're supposed to be in court in twenty-five minutes.'

'Thank you for that, Jan. Could you do me a favour?'

'What?'

'Ring PC Cole at Wells and tell him I want to speak to him about Jake Fayter. Give him my mobile and ask him to ring me, will you?'

'Ask him?'

'No, you're right, tell him to ring me. Thanks.'

Dixon was waiting in the CPS room at Taunton Crown Court when his mobile phone rang.

'You'll remember to switch that thing off when we go in, won't you?'

Dixon didn't recognise the number.

'Nick Dixon.'

'Nick, it's John. John Fayter. I've just had PC Cole on the phone. They want to come today and get some DNA swabs from me and Maureen. What the hell do I tell her?'

'Tell her the truth, John. Maureen's no fool.'

Dixon's prediction had not proved far off the mark and he was back in his office at Bridgwater Police Station by mid-afternoon. A guilty plea to the lesser offence of unlawful wounding had been entered just before lunch but this meant that the hearing had carried over into the afternoon. The offender had been remanded in custody pending sentence and Dixon was not unhappy with the outcome. He could look forward to at least two years with his list of previous convictions.

Operation Magpie was not due to recommence until the following morning, with a briefing scheduled for 9 a.m. sharp.

Dixon thought that he would use the opportunity to look into Jake's death. He remembered that he had not switched his mobile phone back on after the court hearing and did so, only to find that he had missed a call from PC Cole.

He rang Cheddar Police Station.

'This is DI Dixon from Bridgwater CID. Could you put me through to PC Cole, please?'

'Can you hold for a moment, Sir?'

Cole came on the line. 'You're ringing about the climbing accident, Sir?'

'It's nice to know you have an open mind about the cause of death, Constable.'

'Well, it looks like an accident, Sir.'

'Appearances can be deceptive.'

'Sorry, Sir.'

'Do you have any witnesses?'

'We have five members of a coach party down from Birmingham. They've gone back now, so I'll be asking the local force to take statements from them in due course. We have their cameras. They're with the High Tech team now. There are a number of photos, apparently, and one of the witnesses believes that he may have shot a short length of video footage on his digital camera shortly before the fall.'

'Good, can you email the photographs and video to me as soon as you get them?'

'Yes, Sir.'

'Where's his climbing equipment?'

'We have that here.'

'I'd like to have a look at it, so please ensure that it's not disposed of or returned to the family until I get there. Let me have copies of the witness statements as soon as you get them too. Have instructions been given to the Birmingham lot yet?'

'No, not yet. We only completed the identification today. May I ask whether you have any particular interest in the case, Sir?'

'No, you may not. What about the post mortem?'

'Yesterday. Multiple injuries. There wasn't a lot left of him, to be honest, after a fall from that height.'

'So I gather. What time do you shut up shop over at Cheddar this afternoon?'

'I'll be here until 6 p.m. tonight, Sir.'

'In that case, I'll be over before then to have a look at the climbing equipment, if you can have it ready, please.'

'Will do, Sir.'

Dixon called in at his cottage in Brent Knoll for a change of clothes and to pick up Monty before heading over to Cheddar Police Station. PC Cole had Jake's climbing equipment ready on the table in the back office. It consisted of a small rucksack, with two 9 mm ropes attached to it. Both the rucksack and the ropes were spattered with blood. There were also two slings and a screw gate karabiner that had been found still looped around a tree at the top of High Rock.

Dixon looked at the ropes and could see that neither had been cut. He checked the free ends of each rope for damage and could see none. No scuff marks. Nothing.

At the other end, the ropes had been tied together and then attached to the rucksack with another karabiner and a figure of eight knot. The rucksack itself was a small day sack. It had in it a small bottle of Diet Coke that had burst in the fall, a pair of trainers, a pair of jeans with wallet, keys and cash in the pockets, and a lightweight fleece top.

'No phone?'

'No, Sir.'

'Don't you think that's a bit odd?'

'Well, I hadn't really . . .'

'Have you checked his car?'

'No, Sir.'

'Asked his parents?'

'No.'

'Don't you think that might be a good idea?'

'Yes, Sir, I'll get onto it.'

'Where's his harness and Shunt?'

'The harness is at the mortuary, Sir. What's a Shunt?'

'It's a device that moves up a rope but locks under downward pressure. It should have been attached to the harness. It might be an idea if you familiarised yourself with climbing equipment, don't you think?'

'Yes, Sir. It'll be at the mortuary with his harness, I expect. It'll be bagged up and brought over here in due course.'

'Let me know when it is, please, I'd like to have a look at it. And let me know when you find his phone.'

'Yes, Sir.'

Dixon left Cheddar Police Station and drove up the gorge until the cliffs began to tower above him on either side. The early evening sun was striking the tops of the cliffs. He parked in the car park at the bottom of High Rock and could see an area at the base of the cliff still sectioned off with blue tape. There was a large patch of bloodstained sand marking the spot where Jake had landed. He got out of his car, leaned back against the bonnet and looked up.

What the fuck happened, Jake?

Dixon called the meeting to order just after 9 a.m. DS Gorman had read the file over the weekend and so was up to speed on the investigation. Also present was DC Dave Harding. Harding had been a detective constable for twenty years and Dixon reckoned that he would retire a detective constable. He also had the disconcerting habit of wearing a crumpled grey suit and brown suede shoes. Dixon remembered his father always telling him never to trust a man who wore a grey suit and brown suede shoes, although he had been referring to the Chancellor of the Exchequer at the time.

DC Jane Winter was young and keen. She was sitting her sergeant's exams and clearly had her eye on promotion. Dixon was glad to have her on the team. Police Sergeant Wilkins from uniform was also there for liaison. Assistance from uniformed officers would no doubt be needed when the surveillance operation came to a head. Dixon was irritated to see DCI Lewis was also sitting at the back of the incident room listening in.

'There's been another burglary over the weekend. This time in Torquay. I've spoken to the Devon and Cornwall lot this morning. An elderly lady by the name of Avril Wilkins died last Monday and the property was burgled either Saturday or Sunday. The MO is identical to our lot. Nothing of value taken at all and as far as anybody can tell only paperwork is missing.'

'Has the death notice been placed in the paper yet?'

'No, it hasn't, but there lies the key to this whole operation, Steve. In every burglary bar one the break in has taken place before the death notice has been placed in the newspaper, right?'

'That's right, which is why we thought that the two were unconnected.'

'They are connected, Dave, and for this reason. Most of these local newspapers are now weekly papers. In fact, I think they're all weekly papers these days. This means that a death notice placed on a Tuesday, Wednesday, Thursday or Friday will not be published in the paper until the following week. But what was missed before is that the death notice will appear online straight away.'

Dixon paused for effect.

'So, if we look again at the eleven burglaries, all of them took place after the death notice was placed online, in fact within forty-eight hours of it going online, but only one took place after the death notice was published in the newspaper.'

Dixon could see light bulbs coming on around the room.

'This means that the gang's using the online death notices and not those published in the newspaper,' said Dave Harding.

'That's right, and this is why it was missed first time around. Does that make sense to everyone?'

There was a general nodding of heads.

'Jane, what I need you to do is look again at all the witness statements we've got in each burglary and check to see if reference is made to when the death notice was placed online. I'm afraid it may mean taking further witness statements from the funeral directors. Can you get onto that, please?'

'Yes, Sir.'

'So, what we do is place a fake death notice online and wait for them?'

'That was my first thought but it's not quite that simple, Steve.'

'It never is.'

Dixon ignored him.

'I think this gang is too intelligent to fall for that. I certainly wouldn't. At the very least, I'd check with the Land Registry website to see that the deceased is the registered proprietor of the property.'

'Registered proprietor?'

'Owner, you twat, Dave.'

'Thank you for that, Steve.' Dixon continued. 'This means that we're going to need to use a genuine death notice where the deceased was the owner of the property. Steve, can you liaise with funeral directors in, say, Bridgwater and Wells? We're looking for a death where the property has been left unoccupied. Ideally, one where the executors are local solicitors and there's no direct family involved. OK? Ask that they notify us immediately.'

'I'll get onto that straight away.'

'Hopefully, we'll have time to set up surveillance inside the property and around before the death notice is placed online. Assuming all goes to plan, we should have a visit from the gang within two days.'

'Are you proposing to wait inside the property?'

'I don't think so, Dave. It could be a long wait. I suggest we look for a friendly neighbour who might let us sit in an upstairs room overlooking the property. We can have a surveillance van nearby and perhaps even the helicopter on standby?'

Dixon looked towards DCI Lewis, who nodded in agreement.

'I'd suggest having an armed response unit on standby just in case.'

'Thank you, Sir. We'll certainly take you up on that. Any other questions?'

'Have you thought about checking with the Land Registry, Sir, to see if they can tell you who has been searching against the eleven properties burgled so far?' asked Jane.

'I looked at that. I did ask, but the Land Registry told me that they can't help us on that one, at least not officially.'

'Can't or won't?'

'A bit of both, probably, but I'm not too concerned about that. I'd expect this lot to be too savvy to leave that sort of footprint. They're probably using web based email set up via a proxy server and almost certainly a stolen credit card each time to pay the Land Registry fee.'

'Good point, Sir.'

Dave Harding leaned across to Steve Gorman. 'What the hell is a proxy server?'

Dixon ignored it.

'OK, Dave, can you help Jane with the statements from the funeral directors, please? Again, what we're looking for is the date when the notice was sent to the newspapers for publication. It may also mean taking statements from the editors or somebody at the newspaper to confirm when the notice was actually placed online. I reckon it'll prove that the death notice went live on the Internet forty-eight hours before each burglary.'

'Are you keeping Devon and Cornwall in the loop, Nick?' Lewis again.

'Yes, Sir. I'm dropping down to Torquay this afternoon to liaise with the officer investigating down there. They're already looking into when the death notice was placed in the *Herald Express*. It's published every Wednesday and I'm guessing that the death notice went online either Friday or maybe Thursday at the earliest. I'll let you know.'

The team began closing notebooks and gathering up their papers.

'Right then, everybody, if we could meet back here at, say, 6 p.m. this evening. It will then be a matter of waiting for a call from a funeral director. Be aware that when the call comes, we'll have to move pretty damn quick.'

Dixon had only just sat down in his office when DCI Lewis appeared in the doorway.

'Very impressive. Let's hope we get a result.'

'Yes, Sir.'

'I gather you've been asking questions about the climbing accident in Cheddar Gorge last week?'

'Accident?'

'Incident, then.'

'It's my job to ask questions, Sir. Is there a problem?'

'Not as far as I am concerned, no. I'm just wondering why you're so interested in the case.'

'Jake Fayter was my climbing partner for six years before I joined the Met.'

'What I'm not clear about is why you would think it was anything other than a straightforward accident. The ropes had clearly not been cut, so the obvious inference is that the knot came undone?'

'That's not a mistake Jake would have made . . .'

Lewis interrupted. 'Let's look at it another way then. If the knot at the top had been properly tied, there is simply no way that anybody could have undone it with his weight sitting on the ropes, surely?'

'I can think of at least one way straight off the bat.'

'How?'

'Using a second anchor and a clamp fixed to the ropes below the knot to take the weight.'

'Possible but unlikely.'

'It is, Sir, but actually it's far more straightforward than that.' Dixon leaned back in his chair. 'Jake was using the ropes to protect himself while he was practising the moves on a new route. He'd been trying it for nearly two years, according to his parents. They told me that he was very nearly at the point when he was ready for the first ascent, which means that he was able to do all of the moves on the climb.'

'Which means that his weight would have been on the rock face for longer?'

'And off the rope, that's right, Sir. So, assuming Jake was practising one of the easier sequences, his weight could have been off the rope for anything up to five minutes, longer even, which is plenty of time for the knot to have been undone at the top.'

Lewis nodded slowly.

'Not only that but the weight on the end of the rope Jake was using to keep it tight was his small rucksack, which contained just a small bottle of Coke and some clothing.'

'Have you told anybody about this?'

'No, not yet. I'm told that one of the witnesses shot a short section of video footage shortly before the fall and I'm hoping that will show whether Jake was climbing immediately before the fall or whether he was sitting with his weight on the rope. If he was climbing, then his weight would have been off the rope and the knot could have been undone. It's just something that's niggling me, Sir.'

'I can see that. But an accident still remains the most likely explanation.'

'Very possibly, Sir, but I shall keep asking questions until I am satisfied.'

'You do that, Nick. Just try not to ruffle too many feathers.'

It had been a long day. Apart from half an hour on Meadfoot Beach and a quick tour of the Torquay Police Station car park, Monty had spent the rest of the time in the back of the Land Rover. Dixon felt that this was better than leaving him at home on his own all day, particularly given that his tenancy agreement banned pets.

He was back in the incident room at Bridgwater Police Station just after 5.30 p.m. Everyone was there, so he suggested that the day's debriefing start straight away.

'What news? Jane, you first.'

'I've checked with the funeral directors and with the newspapers and, surprise surprise, in each case the death notice went live on the Internet between twenty-four and forty-eight hours before the burglary.'

'Well done, Jane. How have you got on, Steve?'

'I've been in touch with all the funeral directors in Bridgwater and Wells. I included Burnham-on-Sea for good measure, as well. Got a call back within an hour or two from Carters in Bridgwater with an elderly gentleman in Spaxton who died yesterday, apparently.'

'That's good.'

Jane couldn't stifle a laugh and Dixon realised immediately what he had said. 'Well, you know what I mean.'

'I wouldn't get too excited, Sir. I spoke to the solicitor dealing with the estate and he won't cooperate with us. Too worried about getting sued, I expect. It's bloody irritating because the property looks ideal from Google Earth but, instead of playing ball, the jobsworth twat has instructed the funeral directors not to place the death notice at all.'

'Git.'

'Thank you for that, Dave. The news from Torquay is that the burglary took place thirty-six hours after the death notice went online so we're now in a race with Devon to catch these buggers. Let's spread the net a bit wider. We need to get in touch with funeral directors across the whole county. Steve, can you get onto that first thing in the morning?'

'Yes, Sir.'

'Any other developments?'

Silence.

'OK, well if not, let's call it a day and meet back here in the morning. Jane, you will have your work cut out taking new statements from the funeral directors and newspapers, won't you?'

'Yes, I'm going to do the funeral directors and Dave will cover the newspapers.'

'Good. Well, I'll see you all tomorrow.'

Dixon arrived home just after 6.30 p.m. It was too late to take Monty for another walk, so he fed him and then opened a can of beer.

Dixon had always enjoyed a good film. He regarded his favourite films as places to go rather than simply movies to be watched and this evening he fancied a trip to the high seas. He must have seen *Master and Commander* at least fifteen times. In fact, his collection consisted of no more than twenty films but he had watched all of them many times over. He stretched out on the floor in front of the television with Monty curled up beside him, and was asleep before the first cannon shot was fired.

Chapter Three

Dixon was sitting at his desk waiting for the phone to ring when it rang. It was not the call that he had been expecting.

'PC Cole, Sir.'

'Good morning, Constable. I'm assuming you have some news for me?'

'Yes, Sir. I've got Fayter's climbing equipment from the mortuary, or rather his harness and the Shunt thing. They're a bit of a mess, I'm afraid.'

'Anything unusual about them?'

'The harness had been cut off him at the mortuary but apart from that I can see no damage or anything unusual about them at all.'

'Hang onto them for the time being, will you? What about the phone?'

'I've got that too.'

'Where did you find it?'

'I didn't, Sir. It was dropped in by the father.'

'Where did he find it?'

'In the car.'

'Am I to assume from that that you haven't checked the car?'

'No, Sir. It was recovered from the scene direct to the parents' house.'

'Don't you think it might be a good idea to check the car, then?'

'What do you think I might find, Sir?'

'Well, you would have found the phone for starters, wouldn't you?'

'I can check it later on today, if you think it necessary.'

'No, leave it to me. Just make sure that you hang onto the phone until I say so. What is it, by the way?'

'An iPhone, Sir.'

'Any news on the statements from Birmingham?'

'We should have them by the end of the week. I'm expecting the photos from the High Tech Unit later on today or first thing tomorrow.'

'Don't forget to email them straight across to me as soon as you get them, Constable.'

'I won't, Sir.'

Sarah Heath had readily agreed to a meeting when Dixon had telephoned her first thing in the morning, and it was just after 10.30 a.m. when he pulled up outside the address in The Grove, Burnham-on-Sea. He had left strict instructions for Steve Gorman to ring him immediately he received a call from a funeral director.

Dixon guessed that the property was 1930s. It was adjacent to the Avenue Lawn Tennis Club and had clearly been divided into flats. Jake had shared the garden flat with Sarah and this was accessed by a door at the side of the property.

Dixon thought that she was in her early thirties. She had short blonde hair and wore jeans and a white T-shirt but otherwise looked as if she had just got out of bed. At her invitation, Dixon followed

Sarah through to the lounge, which was at the rear of the flat, over-looking the garden.

She offered Dixon coffee, which he accepted, and disappeared into the kitchen to put the kettle on. The kitchen was in a small alcove at the back of the lounge and Dixon could hear Sarah from where he was sitting on the leather sofa. He took a moment to take in the room. There was a large television with a DVD rack next to it. A display of dried flowers told him that the fireplace was not in use. The mantelpiece was covered with photographs and ornaments and an ornate mirror was hanging on the wall above. Otherwise, there was a low three seat sofa that Dixon was sitting on, a glass coffee table with TV and DVD gizmos on it and a small table and chairs against the wall on the opposite side of the room. That would be the dining area.

Dixon noticed immediately that there was not a single trace of Jake in the room. No photographs of him on the mantelpiece, none of his books anywhere nor any of the action films that he knew Jake enjoyed in the DVD collection.

They had exchanged the usual pleasantries when Dixon had first arrived, but Sarah had not said a word whilst she was mak-ing the coffee. Dixon had left her to it. When she reappeared with two mugs of coffee, he took the initiative.

'How long did you know Jake?'

'We met about two years ago when he was still seeing Ruth. I was working in the Clarence. It all got a bit messy for a time. Then he dumped her and moved in with me.'

'Is this your flat then?'

'Yes, well, I rent it. I've lived here about four years now, I think.'

She sat on the floor with her back against the patio window.

'Where are you working now?'

'I'm still at the Clarence.'

'Had Jake moved in full time or was he just staying here from time to time? I don't see any of his stuff around the place.'

'I bagged it all up and dropped it back to his parents yesterday.'

'Why was that, if you don't mind me asking?'

'I do mind you asking.' There was suddenly aggression in Sarah's voice. 'Are you here in an official capacity?'

Dixon kicked himself for the insensitive question.

'No, not at all. I'm just trying to find out what happened to Jake.'

Sarah forced a smile of sorts.

'I'm sorry. It's difficult. He talked about you a lot, you know. The glory days, he used to call them.'

'That they were.'

'He told me about his solo ascent of, what was it, Quiet Waters?'

'He told everyone about that. So, you know why I'm here?'

'Yes, I suppose so.'

'I'm just trying to get to the bottom of what happened. I simply cannot believe that his knot just came undone.'

Sarah looked as if she was about to start crying.

'Was he working?' asked Dixon.

'Not really. Odd jobs for cash, you know. He was claiming Jobseeker's Allowance as well.'

'What sort of cash in hand jobs was he doing?'

'A bit of gardening here and there, the odd bit of labouring. He worked on the roller coaster at the leisure centre too. Nothing regular.'

'Had he been climbing a lot recently?'

'Not a huge amount. He'd been on several trips to Wales with Dan and one trip to Jordan but he wasn't climbing as much as he used to.'

'Jordan?'

'Yes, there's some good climbing out there, apparently. Plenty of new routes to be had, he said.'

'Tell me about Dan.'

'Dan Hunter. His new climbing partner. I didn't know him that well.'

'Did you ever go climbing?'

'Never. Never saw the point in it.'

'You sound like my mum.'

Sarah smiled, stood up and turned to look out of the window. 'Wait a minute,' she said. When she turned round to face Dixon, the smile had gone. 'If you're saying that Jake's knot wouldn't have come undone, are you saying that somebody else undid it? That would be murder, wouldn't it?'

'I'm not saying that, no. I'm just saying that I don't know what happened and I owe it to him to find out. I can't rule out foul play, of course. But, equally, I have no evidence to suggest that it was foul play. Does that make sense?'

'Yes.'

'I don't expect to find anything but I promised Maureen I'd look into it.'

Sarah opened the patio door and stepped into the garden. Dixon followed.

'Do you know anyone who might have had a grudge against him?'

'Of course not.'

'Was he involved in anything he shouldn't have been, Sarah?'

'What do you mean?'

'He was driving a Subaru Impreza. And it's not an old one, as you know. That's a lot of cash in hand and Jobseeker's Allowance, wouldn't you say?'

'Fuck you.'

'Look, this isn't about what Jake was up to. It's about what happened to him. It's about seeing if there's anyone out there who might have a motive to do him harm. OK?'

'Of course there's no one. Don't be so . . .' Her voice tailed off.

30

'What?'

'It's probably nothing.'

'Tell me anyway.'

'The night before he died we were in the Vic. He went outside for a smoke and I could see him arguing with a bloke.'

'Did you ask him what it was about?'

'He wouldn't tell me.'

'Would you recognise the man again?'

'I doubt it. Jake was stood between him and me most of the time.'

'Did you tell PC Cole about this when he spoke to you?'

'He hasn't spoken to me yet. He's spoken to John and Maureen but not me.'

'And you've got no idea who this man was or what the argument was about?'

'No.'

It was a short drive from Sarah's flat in The Grove to Jake's parents' bungalow in Braithwaite Place, but Dixon managed to fit in a telephone call to PC Cole. He told him to take a witness statement from Sarah straight away and, specifically, to get as much information as he could from her about the argument Jake had with an as yet unidentified white male outside the Vic the night before he died. Cole had asked whether he thought the two incidents were connected. Dixon thought that he had been quite restrained in his response, simply reminding Cole that was the purpose of an investigation.

Dixon knocked on the door of the Fayters' bungalow without an appointment. It was just before 11 a.m. and he could see that the Honda Civic was gone from the drive. Jake's Subaru was also missing and he guessed that it was in the garage. John Fayter answered the door.

'Do you have any news, Nick?'

'Nothing substantive, John. I was just passing and wanted to have a word with you, if that's OK?'

'Yes, of course, come in. Maureen's gone shopping.'

They walked through into the kitchen where John had been making a cup of tea.

'Would you like one, Nick?' asked John.

'No, thank you. I've just had a cup of coffee with Sarah.'

'What did she have to say for herself?'

'She saw Jake arguing with a man outside the Vic the night before he died. Do you have any idea what that might have been about?'

'No, no idea. Do you think it might be significant?'

'I don't know at this stage, to be honest. But it's certainly something to be looked into. The first thing we've got to do, though, is find out who Jake was arguing with.'

John finished making his mug of tea. 'Let's go and sit down.'

'Sarah told me that she dropped round all of Jake's belongings yesterday?'

'That's right.'

'A bit quick, wouldn't you say?'

'We thought it a bit odd but people must deal with grief in their own way, I suppose.'

'Would you mind if I had a look at them?'

'Not at all, they're in his room.'

'Do they include his computer?'

'Yes, it's on the bed.'

'Where's his car?'

'I put it in the garage. It kept reminding us what had happened and we wanted it out of the way.'

Dixon nodded.

'It's not that we wanted him out of sight, out of mind,' said John. 'I just felt that Maureen could do without the constant reminder every time she saw the car.'

'I quite understand, John. Can I have a quick look in his room?'

John showed Dixon through to Jake's bedroom. He opened the door and then stepped to one side to allow Dixon into the room. Dixon thought that the room had not changed much since Jake had first left home. In fact, it still looked like a teenager's bedroom. There were climbing posters on the wall above a single bed, a built in wardrobe, a chest of drawers and also what looked like a purpose built computer desk but with no computer on it. A surfboard was leaning against the wall next to the wardrobe and various boxes and bags had been dumped on the bed that Dixon took to be the belongings dropped off by Sarah.

'John, I'm going to need to look through his stuff quite carefully. Do you mind?'

'I quite understand, Nick, you go ahead. I'll be in the living room. Maureen will be back in an hour or so and it'd be nice if you'd finished by then.'

Dixon began by looking through the boxes and bags on the bed. He found Jake's computer and put it to one side, hoping that John Fayter would let him take it with him. Otherwise, there was nothing of interest on the bed. It was just clothing, toiletries and a few CDs and DVDs. Jake had obviously travelled light.

There was still some clothing in the wardrobe but, for the most part, it was full of climbing equipment. Dixon recognised Jake's plastic mountaineering boots, crampons and ice axes. There was also a good selection of winter clothing, mittens and ice climbing gear.

On the floor of the wardrobe was Jake's camping equipment. Dixon could see a tent, sleeping bag and stove. There was also a telescopic golf ball retriever under the bed, which struck him as odd.

Dixon found nothing of interest in the chest of drawers and the computer desk, so he walked back through to the living room where John Fayter was watching the BBC News Channel.

'I didn't know Jake played golf.'

'He didn't,' replied John.

'Do you?'

'No, never have. Why?'

'There's a telescopic golf ball retriever under the bed. Not only that, but it looks like someone has drilled a hole through the handle for some reason. You have any idea what that's all about?'

'None at all. I didn't even know it was there. I'll ask Maureen if she knows anything about it when she gets back.'

'Thanks,' said Dixon. 'Can I have a look in Jake's car while I'm here?'

'Of course. Follow me.'

John Fayter opened the garage door to reveal the silver 2009 Subaru Impreza WRX.

'It was his pride and joy. Capable of nought to sixty in under five seconds, or something like that.'

'It's a nice car. Did you ever ask him how he was able to afford it?'

'No. If he was up to no good, Maureen and I didn't want to know.'

John Fayter handed the keys to Dixon. He climbed into the driver's seat, which was a tight squeeze in the small single garage. John squeezed in alongside the driver's door, so Dixon put the key in the ignition and rolled the window down.

'Jake always used to go for estate cars, if I remember rightly. That way he could sleep in it at night, if he needed to,' said Dixon.

'He was getting on a bit these days, Nick, so he used to stay in bed and breakfasts.'

'I never thought I'd see the day when Jake Fayter stayed in a B&B!'

John managed a small laugh.

'Is the car on HP or anything like that, do you know?' asked Dixon.

'I think he told Maureen he paid cash for it.'

Dixon looked in the door pockets and the glove box but could see nothing unusual. He felt under the seats, but apart from an empty CD box for U2's *Rattle and Hum*, there was nothing. The car was clean and tidy and Dixon reckoned it must have cost Jake well over twenty thousand pounds. He would check later online.

Dixon scrambled out of the driver's seat and went to the rear of the car, where he opened the boot. There were various bits of loose climbing equipment, a spare rope and a helmet. Dixon could never recall Jake ever having worn a climbing helmet in all the years that he climbed with him. He looked quizzically at John.

'It wouldn't have done him much good from that height,' said John.

'Where did you find the phone?'

'It was in the glove box.'

'It's a very nice car. What are you going to do with it?'

'We'll hang onto it for the time being and then sell it, perhaps, when we feel up to it. It's all a bit raw at the moment.'

'Well, there's no rush,' said Dixon, locking the car and handing back the keys. 'I'm hoping to get the photographs and the witness statements from Birmingham shortly. I'll let you know if there's anything interesting in them. Give my regards to Maureen. I'm afraid I must be on my way.'

Dixon's phone rang in his jacket pocket just as he reached out to shake John Fayter's hand.

'Nick Dixon.'

'Steve Gorman, Sir. We've had a call from the Co-op in Burnham. An elderly lady in Axbridge has died. A Mrs Waldron.

The executor is Mr Edwards at Clark and Watts Solicitors and he's happy to help in any way he can.'

'OK, I'll be back in about half an hour. Can you ring Mr Edwards and see if he can see me this afternoon? I'm assuming you asked the funeral director to hold the bereavement notices for the time being?'

'Yes, Sir.'

'Good.'

Dixon rang off. 'I'm afraid I must dash, John.'

They shook hands before Dixon ran over to his car.

Dixon couldn't help but think that Peter Edwards was unduly cheerful for a solicitor specialising in probate work. Edwards had readily agreed to the surveillance operation on the understanding that Mrs Waldron's insurance company was also content for it to proceed. He was awaiting confirmation. In the meantime, Dixon had looked at the property on Google Earth and it seemed ideal. Bridge House was a double fronted Georgian property on the outskirts of the village. There were houses opposite, and the property could be reached across two fields at the rear.

Edwards had confirmed that the property was registered in the names of the deceased and her late husband. He had died in 2008 and the title had not been updated. Perfect.

Gorman was speaking to the neighbours to enquire whether any would be content for a surveillance point to be set up on their property. Otherwise, it was just a matter of waiting for the insurers to confirm they were happy.

Dixon was at the coffee machine when his telephone rang. DI Janice Courtenay picked up for him.

'It's Edwards at Clark and Watts.'

Dixon abandoned his coffee to take the call.

'Insurers are quite happy for the operation to go ahead, Inspector, on the understanding that all damage will be paid for by the police. Is that OK?'

'Yes, it is.'

'In that case, can I leave it to you to liaise with the funeral director over the timing? The placement of the death notice, that is. I've given him the wording to use, and as far as I'm concerned, it can go in whenever you're ready. I've rung him to confirm.'

'Thank you, Mr Edwards. This really is exceptionally helpful.'

'My pleasure, Inspector. Good luck!'

'Thank you.'

Dixon left his office and walked out into the CID room.

'Right then, everyone, we're good to go. Bridge House, Axbridge. Jane, can you liaise with the Surveillance Unit, and Dave, can you get onto Sergeant Wilkins? We'll need some backup on this one. DCI Lewis promised us an armed response unit on standby. Steve, can you get onto them and the helicopter too?'

'A dog unit might be useful, Sir, if we have open fields at the back.'

'Good thinking, Jane. Dave, can you ask Wilkins if he can lay that on for us, please?'

Chapter Four

The team was ready by 9 a.m. the following day. Dixon, Jane Winter and two uniformed police constables were in an upstairs room of the property opposite, overlooking the front of Bridge House. Steve Gorman and Dave Harding, along with two more police constables, had drawn the short straw, quite literally, and were in the stable block at the rear of the property next door. The dog team was in the field directly behind Bridge House.

The front, back and conservatory doors were wired and there were hidden cameras in every room on the ground floor. The surveillance van was parked in a barn on a farm about five hundred yards west of Bridge House.

Dixon confirmed to the funeral director that the bereavement notice could now be placed online, and received a call back within twenty minutes with the news that Mrs Waldron's death notice was now live. It was an interesting choice of words.

'You ever tried fishing, Jane?'

'No, Sir.'

'It's a bit like this, really. Set your bait and wait.'

Dixon's phone rang just after 4.30 p.m. It was the IT manager at HM Land Registry, Plymouth, with unofficial confirmation that the server logs were showing a search against Bridge House, Axbridge, timed at 3.17 p.m. that afternoon. The manager had been at pains to stress that the call had been off the record.

Game on, thought Dixon. He put the team on standby.

It had been dark for about two hours when Dixon noticed a dark blue VW Golf GTI Mark II driving slowly past Bridge House. Dixon had no idea what mark the VW Golf had reached over the years, but he was in no doubt that VW had never been able to improve on the old Mark II.

Three minutes later the VW Golf appeared again, driving in the opposite direction. It pulled up briefly across the driveway to Bridge House and Dixon could see the figure in the driver's seat looking up at the property. It would not be long now.

⌣

Dixon was asleep in the back of his Land Rover with Monty when his radio crackled into life. He checked his watch. It was just after 8 a.m.

He stuffed a handful of fruit pastilles into his mouth and was back upstairs in a matter of seconds to see a white van parked in the driveway of Bridge House. It was signwritten 'RAD Heating & Engineering' and Dixon had arrived in time to see three men in blue overalls climb out of it. He reached for his radio.

'We have a white van out front. Three white males in blue overalls. Let's wait for them to break in and give 'em a few moments to get settled.'

Jane looked at him quizzically. 'Sweets, Sir?'

'Blood sugar.' Dixon grinned.

He watched one of the men ring the front doorbell and wait. One of the other men then went round to the rear of the property and reappeared a few moments later giving a thumbs up signal. All three men then went round to the rear of the property, one of them carrying a bag that he had retrieved from the back of the van.

'All three are going round the back. Get ready. Looks like it'll be back door or conservatory door.'

Less than sixty seconds later, the surveillance team came on the line. 'Back door sensor engaged. Cameras showing three men entering the kitchen.'

'Steve, what can you see?'

Gorman had moved from his position in the stables at the rear of the property next door to a point where he could see through the hedge.

'The back door is open and all three are inside.'

'OK, everyone, get ready to go in three minutes. Three minutes.'

Dixon turned to Jane Winter.

'Armed response?'

'At an incident in Bristol, Sir. Helicopter's on its way down and will be here in about ten minutes.'

'Well, we'll just have to take our chances.'

Dixon was on his feet moving towards the door.

'Jane, you block the driveway with the panda car and follow us in.'

He turned to the two uniformed officers carrying the battering ram.

'We need that door off its hinges pretty damn quick. If any of them are in the front rooms, they'll see us coming. Just get us in there as fast as you can.'

Dixon and the two uniformed officers ran across the road at the front of Bridge House and waited behind the garden wall. Dixon reached for his radio.

'Steve, we're going in. As soon as you hear the front door go, make your move. Surveillance, where are they?'

'Two in the study, can't see the third. The tall one with the goatee is Ray Standish. A real nasty piece of work.'

'Did you hear that, Steve?'

'Yes, Sir.'

Jane Winter appeared, driving the panda car that had been parked around the back of the house opposite. The two uniformed officers raced across the lawn with Dixon right behind them. They reached the front door—unseen, Dixon thought. It was a large and heavy door with stained glass windows but the mortice lock had not been set. One solid blow just above the handle and the Yale lock disintegrated. The door flew open.

Dixon could hear shouting to the rear of the property and the two uniformed officers immediately ran along the hall to the back of the house. He could hear Steve Gorman's voice shouting instructions and the police dog barking. He opened the door to his left and found himself in the dining room. It was empty. He moved back into the hall and opened the door opposite, which led into the living room.

The living room had been knocked through into the kitchen breakfast room, creating a large living space that led through to the back of Bridge House. There was a table and chairs at the rear of the room and a sofa, two armchairs and a large glass topped coffee table at the front. Dixon looked to his left to see a big man in blue overalls running straight at him from the rear of the property. It was Standish. Dixon recognised the glint of a blade in his right hand. He moved between Standish and the door. Standish stopped in front of him, brandishing the knife. Jane appeared in the hallway to his left.

'There's a big difference between burglary and murder, Ray.'

Standish was six feet tall and well over sixteen stone.

'The alternative is that you are killed resisting arrest and I get another medal.'

Standish stepped forward and made a lunge at Dixon across the large glass coffee table. Dixon shouted to Jane to stay back when suddenly Steve Gorman slammed into Standish from behind. Both men crashed through the glass coffee table.

There was a sharp crack and the glass shattered. Splinters flew in all directions. Dixon was able to snatch the knife from Standish's hand, and passed it to Jane. He then helped Steve Gorman to his feet. Standish was going nowhere. He was alive but bleeding profusely from various cuts to his hands and face. Steve Gorman appeared to be remarkably unscathed.

'That was quite some tackle, Steve. Thank you,' said Dixon.

'I'd have got sent off for that back in the old days.'

'Better call an ambulance, Jane. Are you all right, Steve?'

Gorman was examining his elbow.

'Fine, Sir. It's just a scratch, I think.'

'Where are the other two?'

'Dave and the uniformed lads got one and the dog got the other.'

Dixon turned to Standish. He was sitting up.

'Raymond Standish, I am arresting you on suspicion of burglary. You do not have to say anything, but it may harm your defence if you do not mention when questioned something that you later rely on in court. Anything you do say may be given in evidence.'

'Whatever.'

'Now, can someone get him a towel or something to wrap his hands in? We're going to have to pay for this bloody carpet.'

It was early afternoon before Dixon and Gorman got away from Bridge House. Standish had been taken to Weston-super-Mare hospital with two uniformed officers for company. The other two burglars had been taken to Bridgwater Police Station and scenes of crime officers had been and gone. The RAD Heating & Engineering van had been impounded and search warrants were being executed on three residential addresses in Bristol that afternoon. It had been a good result.

Dixon was giving Gorman a lift back to Bridgwater in his Land Rover. He felt that he might have misjudged Gorman.

'Thanks again for dealing with Standish.'

'It was a pleasure, Sir. He and I go way back.'

'How so?'

'When you check his record, you'll see an assault on police a few years ago. The bastard got off with a suspended sentence.'

'You?'

'Yes.'

'What goes around comes around.'

'That it does, Sir.'

Dixon drove down through Axbridge to join the A371.

'Mind if we swing by Cheddar Station on the way, while we're here? They've got a phone there I need to have a look at.'

'Not at all, Sir. Anything interesting?'

'Not really.'

The station was closed so Dixon rang PC Cole on his mobile.

'He'll be back in twenty minutes. Mind if we wait?'

Dixon drove up the gorge and parked below High Rock. Two large birds of prey were flying overhead near the tops of the cliffs on the north side of the gorge.

'Look at them. What are they, hawks of some sort?'

'Peregrine falcons, Sir. There's a pair nesting on Priest Rock.'

Gorman spotted the blood soaked sand at the foot of High Rock.

'You'd have thought they'd have cleaned that up by now.'

'Rotten, isn't it?'

'Still, saved me a shitload of paperwork.'

'Paperwork?'

'Yes, he was a dealer.'

'Who was?'

'The guy who fell. Fayter. I was just about to nick him.'

'Jake Fayter was dealing drugs?'

'Yes, Sir. Not only that. He supplied the ecstasy that killed the Williams girl.'

Jake Fayter . . . dealing drugs . . . killed the Williams girl . . . fuck . . .

Dixon felt sick. His head was spinning. He got out of the Land Rover and walked across to the foot of High Rock. Gorman followed.

'Did you know him, Sir?'

'He was my climbing partner for six years before I joined the Met.'

Dixon dropped Gorman at Bridgwater Police Station and was home by 5 p.m. There was a mountain of paperwork to be done to wind up Operation Magpie but it could wait until tomorrow. He needed time to think.

Chapter Five

Dixon had a restless night and was in his office by 7 a.m. the following morning. He powered up his computer to find two emails from PC Cole. The first attached a number of photographs and a short video clip. The second attached five witness statements that had been scanned into PDF format. Dixon looked first at the witness statements. They were handwritten, all by the same officer, and clearly one who regarded Jake's death to have been a routine climbing accident. The version of events in each statement was almost identical and Dixon suspected that the officer had led the witness through what happened. A statement in which a witness simply has to answer yes or no throughout may be good enough for a coroner but would be nothing like good enough for a murder investigation. The witnesses would need to be interviewed again.

All of the witnesses were agreed that Jake had been climbing at the time the rope fell from the top of High Rock. They also confirmed that Jake hung on for a further two or three minutes after the rope dropped to the ground before he finally fell to his death. Dixon hoped that this would be confirmed in the video footage.

Dixon turned to the other email. There were twenty-seven photographs in all and the video clip. Only three had been taken using a zoom lens. The others had all been taken from the ground looking up and Jake appeared to be a tiny dot high up on the rock face.

The photographer who took the last three pictures had crossed the road and moved a little way up the north side of the gorge to improve the angle. He or she had also zoomed in on Jake as much as possible and he could be seen quite clearly. In the first two photographs, Jake was sitting back on the rope with his feet touching the rock face. He was looking up and Dixon recognised the familiar arm movements that told him Jake was working through the sequence in his mind.

In the third and final photograph, Jake could be seen climbing. It looked to Dixon as though Jake's left hand and left foot were sharing the same hold at the top of a crack and he was reaching out as high as he could up the bulging wall above.

Dixon turned his attention to the video clip and clicked on the movie icon. He could see that the clip was six minutes and thirty-seven seconds in length and without hesitation he clicked 'Play'. It was immediately obvious that the video camera had no zoom lens and the cameraman had clearly done nothing to improve the angle either, filming from the car park at the foot of High Rock. No doubt the High Tech Unit could enhance the film. Jake could be seen on the bulging wall above where the last of the photographs had been taken. The clip began with Jake sitting back on the rope. He placed each of his hands in his chalk bag in turn and then rubbed them together. Then he reached forward with his left hand to take a hold on the rock face. He positioned his feet on footholds and began climbing. Dixon made a note of the time. One minute and twelve seconds.

46

He watched as Jake made four moves in sequence before he stopped for a rest. Dixon could see that Jake's weight was still on the rock. He was resting each arm in turn and could also be seen shifting his weight from his left foot to his right and then back again. Dixon thought they must have been better holds enabling Jake to stay in balance.

Suddenly, Jake looked up. Dixon could see the rope falling from the top of High Rock and made a note of the time. Three minutes and forty-two seconds.

Dixon watched as Jake hugged the rock face. The rope fell past him and Dixon could see it was trailing over his back. He watched as Jake released the Shunt and the rope and rucksack fell to the ground. He could see Jake looking up, clearly intending to try to climb out, but for some reason Jake didn't move. Dixon couldn't see why from this distance and made a mental note to get the video footage enhanced.

Then Jake fell. Thankfully, the camera turned away. The film ended at six minutes thirty-seven seconds. Dixon could feel tears streaming down his cheeks.

By 9 a.m. he had watched the video footage four more times. Jake's weight had been off the rope for two minutes and thirty seconds before it fell from the top of High Rock. This would have offered plenty of time for the knot to have been undone. Something else had struck Dixon as a bit odd, although it hadn't occurred to him until his last look at the film. There was no shout or cry for help from Jake at all. Not even when he fell. Dixon wondered whether the camera microphone had not picked it up but no doubt the High Tech Unit could confirm.

He made himself a coffee and sat down to watch the last sequence frame by frame.

Each click of the mouse advanced the film one frame at a time. He had scrolled forward to the point just before the rope came down and looked at each frame intently from that point onwards. He could see Jake resting his left leg, no doubt trying to fight the shakes. Otherwise, the exercise revealed nothing of interest except the fact that Jake never once looked down. The fall, when it came, appeared graceful. Dixon suspected that Jake had reached the point when he knew that he could hang on no longer and gave up the fight. He had experienced that for himself on more than one occasion.

Dixon watched as the camera turned away from High Rock. He kept clicking, taking the film forward frame by frame, as the camera panned sharply to the right taking in the top of Priest Rock, then blue sky until finally the cliffs on the north side of the gorge came into view. Dixon froze. He wound the film back ten or so seconds and then began to take it forward again frame by frame. He could not be sure what it was that he had seen but he needed a closer look.

There it was. A figure standing at the right hand end of the terrace at the foot of Heart Leaf Bluff, the top tier of three on the north side of the gorge. Dixon could just make out a blue top and then, thirty feet above, a climber. They appeared to be doing a route called Dinner Date, which he knew well. It had been his first lead.

Dixon would need to get this frame blown up by the High Tech Unit but the significance of it was clear. He would need to check, of course, but as far as he could recall anyone standing on the terrace below Heart Leaf Bluff would have a clear view of the top of High Rock.

Dixon wondered what efforts PC Cole had made to trace any other witnesses in the gorge that day and immediately left a message at Cheddar Police Station for him to ring straight away. Those climbers had to be traced.

Dixon looked again at the witness statements. None made reference to any climbers on the north side of the gorge. He made a note that those witnesses would need to be spoken to again. He was just about to telephone Cheddar Police Station again when DCI Lewis appeared in the doorway.

'A good result yesterday.'

'It was, Sir, thank you.'

'I gather that Gorman was the hero of the hour?'

'He was. I certainly wouldn't want to have been opposite him in the scrum.'

'It must be the low centre of gravity. It was excellent work though, Nick, well done.'

'Thank you, Sir.'

'Any progress on the Cheddar incident?'

'It turns out that Jake Fayter had been dealing ecstasy, Sir. Gorman was just about to arrest him for supplying the ecstasy that killed the Williams girl.'

'Fuck me.'

'Not only that, but the film footage taken on the day shows climbers high up on the north side of the gorge. They would have had a clear view of the top of High Rock at precisely the time Jake's rope failed.'

'You need to find those witnesses sharpish.'

'I do.'

'Anything else?'

'The film also shows Jake's weight off the rope for two minutes and thirty seconds at the critical time. That's plenty of time for the knot to have been undone.'

'And you have a possible motive if he killed Jenna Williams.'

'I do, Sir, yes. I need access to the Williams file in the first instance.'

'I'll speak to Gorman. Need anything else?'

'Not at this stage. Just some time, really.'

'Well, subject to anything else coming in and finishing off Operation Magpie, of course, take as long as you need.'

———

Dixon overheard the conversation between DCI Lewis and DS Gorman.

'That case is closed, Sir.'

Dixon could not hear the response.

'How can it possibly be relevant to a simple climbing accident in Cheddar Gorge?'

Dixon heard the parting shot from DCI Lewis.

'Just give him the file, Steve, and give it to him now.'

———

It was mid-morning before PC Cole called back. Dixon explained the need to enhance the video footage and the three photographs that had been taken with the zoom lens. Dixon also asked what efforts were being made to trace other witnesses in the gorge.

'None, Sir'

'Well, you'd better get onto it, Constable. The video clip shows two climbers high on the north side of the gorge. They would've had a clear view of the top of High Rock. We need to speak to them.'

'I'll get onto that straight away, Sir. I'll place the usual roadside signs and get an appeal in the local paper.'

'Climbers will travel from miles around to climb in the gorge this time of year. Get in touch with the main climbing magazines and websites. I'll get onto the various climbing clubs and forums and see if they can help.'

'Right.'

'Are there any other photographs?'

'None that are relevant, Sir.'

'Any others taken in the gorge at all?'

'Some, but they don't show Fayter.'

'Maybe not, but they may show cars parked and one of those cars may belong to the climbers we need to speak to.'

'I understand, Sir.'

'Make no mistake about it, the video clip shows that Jake Fayter's weight was off the rope for two and a half minutes just before he fell. That's plenty of time for the knot to have been undone. He was also the main suspect in the death of Jenna Williams.'

'The ecstasy overdose?'

'Yes.'

Dixon spent the next half an hour leaving posts on various Internet forums asking for anyone climbing in the gorge at the time of the fall to contact the police. There was a flurry of responses from concerned climbers, some of whom said they knew Jake, but nothing positive straight away. Dixon subscribed to each thread so he would get an email alert when any further comments were left.

Dixon let his mind wander back to his ascent of Dinner Date. Jake had been holding his ropes, of course. It had been Dixon's first route in Cheddar Gorge. It was a short single pitch route but it felt as if you were stepping off the edge of the world. From the end of the terrace it was exposed to the full height of the gorge almost immediately. Dixon had not read the guidebook properly either and had climbed past the belay point and topped out. He found out later that there were rare orchids on the top of the cliffs but he didn't think that he had trodden on anything precious.

Dixon spent the rest of the day interviewing Standish and his two cronies. Standish looked faintly ridiculous covered in bandages and plasters and it had taken the hospital over fifty stitches to sew him up. The interview proved to be unproductive with Standish answering 'no comment' to each and every question.

The interviews with the other two burglars had proved to be more worthwhile. Both made full admissions detailing a string of burglaries, which matched those under investigation. It included the burglary in Torquay, as well as two others of which the team had not been aware.

The search warrants in Bristol had turned up a significant volume of paperwork from each burglary. A number of computers had also been seized and these were with the High Tech Unit for examination. There remained a good deal of work to be done to prepare the case for future court hearings and this would no doubt keep the team busy for the next few weeks. Dixon would need to supervise this process, of course, but assuming nothing else came in, he would have plenty of time to look into Jake's death.

It was late afternoon before Dixon got back to his desk. He found the Williams case file waiting for him.

Jane Winter appeared in the doorway.

'At Bridge House, Sir, you used the words "another medal"?'

'Just a turn of phrase, Jane. Don't worry about it.'

Gorman appeared in the doorway behind Jane, who took her cue to leave.

'You're wasting your time with that,' said Gorman, pointing to the Williams file.

'Maybe, but I'm investigating the death of the prime suspect. I'd be negligent if I didn't at least read the file, don't you think?' replied Dixon.

'I suppose so but you'll see it was pretty clear cut. A witness saw Fayter give her the drugs and an hour later she was dead.'

'Leave it with me, Steve. I'll let you have the file back in the morning. Maybe we can have another chat about it then? I've had enough for today, I think.'

Dixon took the Williams file home with him. It was dark by the time he reached his cottage so Monty would have to be content with a walk around the roads followed by twenty minutes in the Red Cow. Dixon had always thought it a little odd that he did his best thinking when he was doing something else. Driving and walking his dog were always the most productive. Walking with a Staffordshire terrier always afforded him plenty of time to think because other dog walkers would invariably give them a wide berth. Not that Monty was aggressive, of course, but people always assumed that he was.

Twenty minutes in the Red Cow turned into an hour and a half. Dixon managed to get in a couple of beers and a plate of ham, egg and chips. He was back home by 8 p.m. He opened a can of beer and sat on the floor with the Williams file. He made a mental note to get himself an armchair as soon as possible.

The file itself was comparatively thin. There were statements from the parents of the dead girl, a post mortem report and five from people in the nightclub at the time. Two girls had been with Jenna Williams on an evening out: Lisa Doe and Kelly Sanders. Dixon read their statements first. Both denied any knowledge of drug taking on Jenna's part but otherwise gave a detailed description of the events leading up to her death. It was only afterwards, apparently, that Lisa and Kelly found out that Jenna had been taking drugs.

Of the other three witness statements, two were from staff at the nightclub who gave details of the drinks consumed by Jenna and her friends. Dixon did not think them excessive. He then turned to the post mortem report, which confirmed that Jenna had died from an overdose of PMA, a refined and infinitely more potent form of ecstasy. Dixon had come across it in London and knew it to be far more dangerous than standard ecstasy. The last statement came from a Conrad Benton who saw Jake supply the drugs to Jenna.

Benton's statement represented the only evidence of any wrongdoing on Jake's part. He had been outside the nightclub at the time, smoking a cigarette, when he saw Jake hand to Jenna Williams a small clear plastic bag and receive what looked to be two ten pound notes in return. On the face of it, this was clear evidence of a drug deal taking place. The identification was sound too. Benton and Jake had been at school together. Both had attended King Alfred's Comprehensive School in Burnham-on-Sea in the early nineties, and although they were not in the same year, they had been at the same school for three years. Benton was two years below Jake.

What troubled Dixon was that Benton's statement was dated three weeks before Jake's death. An identification parade would not have been required and Dixon could not understand why Jake had not been arrested straight away. Perhaps Gorman had been looking for some corroborating evidence for Benton's story but Dixon thought that, at the very least, Jake should have been interviewed under caution. He would need to check this with Gorman in due course. He would also need to check whether Benton had a police record before paying him a visit.

Dixon knocked on the door of the Fayters' bungalow in Braithwaite Place just after 10 a.m. the following day. He had taken the precaution of ringing ahead to ensure that Maureen Fayter would be out. He had also arranged for a police dog handler to meet him at the bungalow.

'Still digging, Nick?'

'I am. And I'm afraid you're not going to like what I'm finding, John. What time will Maureen be back?'

'Not until late afternoon. She's gone shopping with a friend in Bath.'

'Good. First things first. I left Jake's computer on his bed last time I was here. Would you mind if I take it? I need to get the High Tech Unit to have a look at it.'

'No, of course. You take it.'

'Is Jake's car still in the garage?'

'Yes.'

'Would you mind if we reversed it out into the driveway? I didn't mention when we spoke earlier but I've arranged for a police dog handler to come and he'll need room to manoeuvre.'

'Police dog handler? Is it a sniffer dog? Please tell me Jake wasn't dealing drugs.'

'It's starting to look that way, John,' replied Dixon.

'Christ, no. What am I going to tell Maureen? We knew he was no saint but . . .'

John's voice tailed off.

'I'm afraid things are going to get worse before they get better.'

'What was it? Please tell me it's not heroin.'

'At this stage, it looks like ecstasy. But I can't really say more now.'

John looked as if he was about to throw up.

'How about we get his car out? Where are the keys?'

John fetched the car keys and went round to the front of the garage. He opened the door, squeezed in along the side of the Subaru and climbed into the driver's seat just as the police dog van arrived and parked across the driveway.

John reversed the Subaru into the driveway and switched off the engine. He looked at Dixon, clearly unsure what to do next.

'Why don't you go in, John? We'll be a minute.'

John nodded. He handed the keys to Dixon and went inside the bungalow. The police dog handler went round the car opening all the doors and the boot. He went to the back of his van reappearing a few moments later with a liver and white springer spaniel. He let the dog off the lead and watched with Dixon while the dog covered the whole car inside and out. The dog appeared to pause on the back seat of the Subaru and then continued sniffing all over the passenger compartment. It spent several minutes in the boot of the car before returning to the back seat, where it sat barking at the rear seat armrest.

'Looks like we have a result, Sir.'

The dog handler put the springer spaniel back on the lead and went to put him back in the van.

'We may need him again in a minute. I'd like him to have a look in one of the bedrooms.'

'OK, Sir.'

Dixon sat on the passenger seat and pulled down the armrest. It had been hollowed out. It appeared normal from the passenger compartment, but when lowered it revealed a Perspex box with two small holes in the top and side. The box had been set into the armrest. The inside of the box had been divided into four compartments, each divided horizontally. The compartments were lined with foam. There was also a switch wired up to a small light bulb. Both had been taped to the inside of the Perspex box. Dixon realised he was looking at an incubator.

'Any luck, Sir?'

Dixon had found four small plastic bags each containing two pink tablets on the bottom shelf of the rudimentary incubator. He passed them out to the dog handler.

'Ecstasy, Sir?'

'PMA.'

'What's that?'

'Think ecstasy, only stronger and far more dangerous.'

'I've not come across it before,' said the dog handler, as he placed each of the four plastic bags into a large evidence bag.

'There's a lot of it about in London.'

Dixon sat on the rear passenger seat for several minutes, his mind racing. An incubator could mean only one thing. Eggs. And the need to keep those eggs alive. Dixon jumped out of the car and ran into the bungalow.

'John, do you mind if I have another look in Jake's room?'

'No, you go ahead.'

Dixon went into Jake's bedroom and looked under the bed. The telescopic golf ball retriever was still there.

He poked his head around the sitting room door.

'Mind if we get the dog to sniff around Jake's room?'

'You do what you have to do.'

Dixon went outside and placed Jake's computer and the telescopic golf ball retriever on the front seat of his Land Rover. He then motioned to the dog handler to follow him into the bungalow. They repeated the same procedure with the springer spaniel in Jake's bedroom. This time there was no result.

The dog handler left taking the eight tablets, which would need to be booked in back at Bridgwater. Dixon went into the sitting room.

'I think we need to have a chat, John.'

John Fayter took the news badly that his son had been a small time drug dealer and illegal birds' egg collector. He found the drug dealing more difficult to come to terms with than the egg collecting. Dixon did not mention that Jake was suspected of having supplied the fatal dose that killed a teenage girl at a nightclub in Bridgwater.

He felt sure that John and Maureen Fayter would find this out for themselves in due course, and they had enough to deal with at this stage.

Dixon explained that the car would need to be impounded for forensic examination. John Fayter put it back in the garage, locked it and gave both sets of keys to Dixon.

'What about his death, Nick?'

'At this stage, I'm still looking for a motive. Although I'm thinking I may have found two possibilities.'

'Drug dealing and egg collecting?'

'Yes. I've had the photographs and video footage from the tourists and they prove that Jake's weight was off the rope long enough for the knot to have been undone. That's if it was undone. I still have no real evidence that it was anything other than an accident.'

'I don't know what the hell I'm going to tell Maureen.'

Flat 4, Burnham-on-Sea High Street turned out to be above Roly's Fudge Shop and was accessed via a metal staircase at the rear. It was just after 11 a.m. when Dixon rang the doorbell. He could hear music playing and rang again when there was no answer. The door was eventually opened by a small man with short blonde hair and a spider tattoo on his neck. He wore crocs, tight jeans and a white collarless shirt.

'Conrad Benton?'

'Who wants to know?'

'Detective Inspector Dixon, Bridgwater CID.'

'I'm Benton. You'd better come in.'

The flat opened into a small hallway and then, from there, into a large open plan living area that extended the full length of the building. There was a kitchenette along the rear wall with a table and chairs against the wall to the left and then the sitting room area. Three steps led up into the bedroom at the front.

Benton turned the music down.

'I wanted to talk to you about the death of Jenna Williams.'

'I gave a statement about that.'

'You did, but I just want to go over it with you again.'

'If you must. I thought Jake was dead, though?'

'Just tying up a few loose ends, Conrad, if that's OK with you?'

'Fire away.'

'When was the last time you saw Jake before that night at Rococo's?'

'I don't know exactly. I saw him from time to time. Burnham-on-Sea is a small place.'

'How well did you know him?'

'Just to say hello to, really. He wasn't a friend or anything like that.'

'You were at school together. Is that right?'

'Yes, we were both at King Alfred's. He was two years above me.'

'Did you have much to do with him at school?'

'No, not really.'

'Where was Jake standing when he handed the envelope to Jenna Williams?'

'They were in the alleyway at the side of Rococo's.'

'Had you seen Jake in the club earlier that evening?'

'No, he hadn't been in.'

'What was he wearing?'

'God, I can't remember that. Jeans and a leather jacket, I think, I don't know. What does it matter?'

'How did you know it was Jake in the alleyway?'

'As soon as he finished with the girl he walked out into the street. It's well lit at the front of Rococo's and I could see him as plain as day.'

'What about Jenna Williams?'

'She followed a few seconds later.'

'So, if it was dark in the alleyway, Conrad, how did you know a deal had just been done?'

'Because Jake was stuffing the money in his pocket and the Williams girl still had the bag in her hand.'

'Did you know Jenna Williams?'

'No, I didn't find out who she was until later.'

'I'm assuming you identified her from a photograph, then?'

'Yes.'

'One last thing. Did you tell Jake you'd sold him PMA?'

'What the . . . ?'

'Don't fuck with me, Conrad. You have a string of convictions for possession and supplying class A and B drugs. You were Jake's wholesaler. Right?'

'Wrong. I've been clean for fucking ages. Now piss off out of it.'

'PMA is serious stuff, and if I find out you've been pushing it, I'll be all over you like a rash.'

Dixon paused on the landing of the metal staircase outside Benton's flat. Oddly enough, he believed Benton, at least insofar as Jake had supplied the fatal dose to Jenna Williams. He didn't believe the line that Benton was clean and suspected that he had supplied Jake with the drugs shortly before Jake had passed them on to Jenna Williams, but that didn't alter his gut feeling that it was Jake who had supplied the fatal dose. He looked at his watch. Time for a walk on the beach.

Benton waited until he was sure that Dixon had gone before he reached for his phone. He was shaking.

'I just had some copper called Dixon here asking questions.'

'What did you tell him?'

'Nothing. I stuck to my statement.'

'Then you have nothing to worry about.'

'He knows I supplied the drugs to Fayter, that I was his fucking wholesaler.'

'He's not interested in that. He's investigating Fayter's death, which we know was an accident. So just forget it.'

Then the line went dead.

Chapter Six

Dixon was back in his office at Bridgwater Police Station by lunchtime. He locked Jake's computer in the bottom drawer of his desk and put the golf ball retriever in the corner of his office behind his filing cabinet. He decided to spend the rest of the afternoon catching up with Operation Magpie. He was pleased to see that the investigation was coming together nicely. Raymond Standish and his two accomplices had been remanded in custody. The three computers and other documents recovered during the raids in Bristol had provided plenty of evidence of the burglaries themselves and subsequent identity thefts. Standish and the others would face multiple counts of burglary, theft and deception. It would make for a long indictment.

Dixon spent the rest of the afternoon on his own witness statement. This was going to be a long job and would not be completed in one sitting. He was not aware of the time until his phone rang just before 5 p.m.

'There's a Carl Harper on the line for you, Sir. Says he's responding to a post you left on a web forum the other day.'

Dixon paused until he heard the usual click.

'Detective Inspector Nick Dixon speaking. Can I help you?'

'Yeah, my name is Carl Harper. You left a post on the UKClimbing forum asking about the accident in Cheddar Gorge a couple of weeks ago?'

'Yes, that's right.'

'I was there. I was climbing in the gorge that day with my girlfriend, Helen.'

'Did you see the fall?'

'No, I was climbing at the time. I heard the screams and turned round to see the guy land. Poor bastard.'

'What about Helen?'

'She saw much the same as me. She was holding my ropes and watching me at the time. Or at least she bloody well should've been!'

'Do you live locally?'

'No, we live in London. Well, Surbiton, actually. We're members of the Surbiton and Kingston Mountaineering Club. Helen's parents live in Wells, so we come down and stay with them. We're driving down tomorrow night as it happens. The weather forecast looks good for the weekend.'

'I'd like to have a word with you both, Carl, if I may. You'll be in the gorge Saturday?'

'Yes, we will.'

'Could you both spare me half an hour at, say, 9 a.m. I don't want to ruin your day but I really do need to get a clear understanding of what you saw.'

'No problem at all.'

'Thank you. Could we meet at the foot of High Rock, perhaps? In the car park.'

Carl Harper agreed, and Dixon made a note of his full name, address and telephone numbers.

'One final question.'

'Yes?'

'What route were you on?'

'Dinner Date.'

'I'll see you Saturday, Carl.'

Dixon looked at his watch. It was just after 5.30 p.m. Just enough daylight left for a walk on the beach at Burnham and then a beer in the Clarence.

———

Dixon parked at the end of Allandale Road and walked towards the town. He would usually walk in the other direction, towards the lighthouse, but tonight was different. Monty was tearing up and down in pursuit of his tennis ball. He still hadn't got the hang of bringing it back but he made short work of catching it when Dixon kicked it along the beach.

Dixon walked until the new sea defences reared up like a huge wave above him. He still thought of them as new even though they had been built over twenty-five years ago. He remembered the storm that had destroyed the old Esplanade. He walked as far as the second set of steps, put Monty on his lead, and walked onto the top of the sea wall to find himself opposite the Royal Clarence Hotel. He had taken the precaution of checking that Sarah Heath would be behind the bar that evening.

Very little appeared to have changed in the ten years since Dixon was last in the Clarence. To his left was the lounge bar and to his right the public bar. Straight ahead he could see the manager's office, currently occupied, with the passage leading through to the toilets at the rear of the building. To the left of the manager's office was a doorway, which Dixon remembered led up to the guest accommodation.

He walked into the public bar and could see that the whole far end had been opened out to create additional seating and a games area with two pool tables and a dartboard. Gone was the old skittle alley. Sarah was behind the bar to his left. She did not look pleased to see him.

'Got time for a chat, Sarah?'

'No. I'm on my own.'

'I saw the manager sitting in his office when I came in.'

'That's the owner.'

'He won't mind covering the bar for ten or fifteen minutes.'

'What do I tell him?'

'You tell him that there's a police officer here wanting a quick chat with you in relation to the death of your boyfriend. If it's a problem, I could have a word with him.'

'No, it's no problem. Give me a minute.'

Sarah reappeared a few moments later.

'That's fine. I've got fifteen minutes.'

'Would you like a drink?'

'I'll have a small lager, if you don't mind.'

'Not at all.'

Sarah poured the drinks, a small lager for herself and a beer for Dixon, and they both sat in the window where the jukebox had once been.

'Did you know Jake was dealing drugs?'

Sarah hesitated. Dixon waited.

'Yes, ecstasy.'

'Where was he getting them from?'

'Some bloke he had known since school.'

'Name?'

'He never told me his name.'

'Where does he live?'

'Above a shop in the High Street, I think.'

'So, we've got possession with intent to supply a Class A drug.'

'It was only a little bit here and there. Small time for pocket money, really.'

'How much was he making?'

'I told you, just a bit of extra cash. Nothing serious. He'd buy ten pills for fifty quid and sell them on for a hundred. It really wasn't anything.'

'I understand that, Sarah. My only interest in this is purely as a possible motive for his murder.'

'I know, I know.'

'Did you know he was supplying PMA too?'

'No.'

'You know what PMA is?'

'Yes.'

'Did you ever meet his supplier?'

'No.'

'Could it have been the man Jake was arguing with outside the Vic the night before he died?'

'I'd definitely not seen that man before. It could've been him, I suppose.'

'So, he's dealing a bit of ecstasy here and there for extra cash. He's doing the odd bit of cash in hand work and getting, what, Jobseeker's Allowance?'

'Yes.'

'So where did all his money come from?'

'What money?'

'The Subaru?'

'Look, I've got no idea, OK?'

'Tell me about the climbing trip to Jordan. When was it?'

'April, I think. Over Easter.'

'Who did he go with?'

'Dan.'

'How long was he away?'

'It was a week. Just a week.'

'When did he buy the Subaru?'

'I don't know.'

'I can check with the DVLA.'

'May. He got it in May.'

'Tell me about his climbing trips before he went to Jordan, then. Where did he go?'

'He had a couple of weekends in Wales, I think, and went to the Lake District a couple of times as well. The weather wasn't great then, of course.'

'What about when he got back from Jordan?'

'Not a lot after that until the season opened at Cheddar Gorge. Then he started working on As the Crow Flies again.'

'OK, so we've got a couple of trips to Wales, a couple of trips to the Lake District and then he goes to Jordan. Then, when he comes back, he buys the Subaru.'

'What do you think he was up to then?'

'I know full well what he was up to, Sarah. I'm just waiting for you to tell me.'

'I don't know.'

'Did he make any alterations to the car when he got it?'

'What?'

'Alterations to the car. Modifications. Did he make any?'

'Yes, he was mucking about with wires and things in the back seat.'

'Didn't you ask him what he was doing?'

'No, it was none of my business.'

'OK, I'll tell you what I think Jake was up to and you tell me if you think any of this sounds familiar. The climbing trips to Wales and the Lake District weren't climbing trips at all. He was collecting birds' eggs. Let me rephrase that. He was stealing birds' eggs.'

'Bullshit.'

'I found a telescopic golf ball retriever in his bedroom at his parents' house. It had a hole drilled in the handle so that it could be hung on his harness. I'm thinking that the eggs were stolen from peregrine falcon nests and if you can keep them alive, each egg is worth about seven thousand pounds in the Middle East. Now, how am I doing?'

Sarah stared at her drink. She didn't respond.

'That explains the trip to Jordan, doesn't it?'

Sarah nodded.

'Did he really go to Jordan or was it somewhere else? Dubai, perhaps?'

Sarah sighed.

'I can find out, Sarah, so it will save us all a great deal of time.'

'They went to Dubai.'

'How many eggs were there?'

'Ten.'

'Seventy grand?'

'He split it with Dan.'

'Cash?'

'Yes.'

'Who organised it?'

'What you mean?'

'Jake could collect the eggs and keep them alive but he's not going to know anybody in Dubai to sell them to, is he? Who was his contact? Who set it up?'

'I don't know.'

'He never mentioned anyone?'

'No.'

'And you heard no phone calls or anything like that?'

'No.'

'How about the Internet?'

'Could be, I suppose.'

'How did he keep the eggs alive?'

'He had a small plastic box. It had a tiny light bulb in it that was wired up to a small battery pack.'

'It's called an incubator, Sarah.'

'I know.'

'There was one set into the rear seat armrest of the Subaru.'

'He wired it up to the car battery. Even fitted an on-off switch. He was pleased with himself for that.'

'So he was planning to do it again?'

'Yes, when he got back. He said the birds should have laid again by then. He was going to try for twenty eggs but something went wrong. He didn't go.'

'To Dubai?'

'Dan went on his own.'

'They collected the eggs and then Dan took them to Dubai without Jake?'

'Yes.'

'One hundred and forty thousand pounds. More than enough motive for murder, wouldn't you say?'

'I suppose so.'

'So you have no idea who his contact was or how he got in touch with them?'

'No.'

'Did he ever tell you any of his passwords? Facebook, perhaps?'

'No, he kept that sort of information to himself. I never knew any of his passwords and he never knew any of mine.'

'I'm sure our High Tech Unit will be able to sort it out. I've got his computer and iPhone.'

Tears had started to stream down Sarah's face. Dixon noticed that she had not touched her drink.

'Am I in trouble?' she asked.

'No, Sarah. You're not.'

———⌣———

Dixon walked along the seafront towards the amusement arcade. He bought some chips, gave them a liberal covering of salt and vinegar, and then walked down the ramp towards the beach. He sat on the concrete steps below the sea wall and watched the lights flickering on Hinkley Point across the estuary. He could see the marker flashing on the sandbank of Stert Island. The South Wales coast was visible in the distance and he could even pick out the street lighting on the M4. He looked up at the lights flashing in the arcade and his mind wandered back to many an hour spent playing the fruit machines.

'Fruit machines? You might as well go and push your money through their bloody letterbox,' his grandmother had said.

He remembered Jake's ascent of the sea wall too. Using only the tiny crack between the huge sections of concrete wall for finger and footholds, Jake had got up and over the overhang. It was made all the more impressive by the quantity of beer Jake had drunk that evening too. Happy days.

A sense of frustration overtook him. Or was it sadness? He wasn't sure. He was not convinced that he was making any progress at all with his investigation into Jake's death. He was yet to find any evidence that it was anything other than a simple accident. He was finding plenty of evidence to blacken Jake's character, and despite their protestations to the contrary, he was under no illusion that John and Maureen Fayter would thank him for that. But he was no nearer to finding out what had happened to Jake. Something was niggling him. It was irritating him like an itchy scab and he was determined to keep picking at it.

Dan Hunter held the key, Dixon was sure of that. No doubt he would meet him at Jake's funeral tomorrow. Hunter had a great many questions to answer on his own account. Even assuming he was not involved in Jake's drug dealing, he was certainly up to his neck in the theft and sale of the birds' eggs. Dixon made a mental note to have a look at the various offences under the Wildlife and Countryside Act and their sentences. He had no intention of arresting Hunter at this stage but it might be useful to put the wind up him if needs be. Much would depend on whether or not he cooperated. Funerals in murder cases were always interesting and Jake's was likely to be no exception.

Chapter Seven

Dixon never understood why crematoriums all looked the same. He had been to any number of funerals over the years and Weston-super-Mare crematorium was just like any other.

He had arrived early and met Dan Hunter amongst the usual throng waiting patiently in the car park. He explained that he was investigating Jake's death and would need to speak to him in due course. Hunter had asked the 'do you think he was murdered' question that everybody seemed to have asked and to which Dixon gave his stock reply. Much to Dixon's surprise, Hunter had then readily agreed to help in any way he could.

'You know he was dealing drugs?' asked Hunter.

'Yes, small time, I'm told.'

'I wonder whether that could be related though, if he was murdered, that is?'

'It's certainly one line of enquiry but we have several at the moment and, as I say, I have no real evidence that he was murdered. All I have is the knowledge that his knot wouldn't just untie itself.'

Hunter agreed to call into Bridgwater Police Station after work on Monday to give a statement and Dixon felt that questions about the birds' eggs could wait until then. They exchanged mobile phone numbers and Dixon left it at that.

Hunter seemed an odd choice for a climbing partner. Dixon guessed that he was in his early forties, and a generous assessment was that he was not particularly athletic. He had admitted, much as Dixon had to, that he had spent most of his time holding Jake's ropes. He added that they had not climbed much together in recent months but he had known Jake was getting close to a first ascent of As the Crow Flies.

Dixon was standing with Hunter at the back of the crematorium when Jake's coffin was brought in. Jake's parents were walking slowly behind it with Sarah. John Fayter's military bearing appeared to have deserted him and all three were crying.

Dixon couldn't help a wry smile when the congregation started singing 'Rock of Ages', and he wondered whether Jake had told his parents that he wanted 'Never Mind the Bollocks' by the Sex Pistols played at his funeral. It had been their standing joke.

Sarah Heath was dressed in a dark suit and had been doing a good deal of crying. Dixon spoke briefly to John and Maureen Fayter after the service, simply to pass on his condolences. He excused himself from the wake with the explanation that he had to be back at work, and assured them that he would ring them later.

⌣

Dixon was in the gorge by 8 a.m. the following morning. It was pouring with rain. So much for Carl Harper's weather forecast. He had lost count over the years of the number of climbing trips cancelled due to poor weather forecasts. It was similar to the number of trips that turned out to be a total washout after perfect forecasts.

He parked his Land Rover on the verge opposite the car park at the foot of High Rock. Two climbers were about to embark on

Coronation Street despite the weather and he didn't want to take the chance of falling rocks hitting the car. Not that anyone would notice from the bodywork but he had decided to leave Monty in the back. He knew from experience that dogs and cliffs do not mix.

Dixon was wearing an old pair of jeans, trainers, a pullover and a waterproof top. He had with him a small blue rucksack that contained waterproof trousers, a bottle of water, his camera and a pair of binoculars that he had got for five pounds when filling up with petrol many years before. They had proved invaluable ever since. He walked down the gorge to a sharp left hand bend where a small path left the road and crossed the bank on the right. It ran up to the left of the terraces on the north side of the gorge. He knew from experience, of course, that this was the path to the terrace at the foot of Heart Leaf Bluff. He wanted to get a clear idea of what Carl Harper and his girlfriend could have seen before questioning them.

The path rose up sharply and zigzagged over the first broken terrace. It was narrow, more of a sheep run, and covered in loose stones. Dixon followed a fork in the path to the right, which took him out along the terrace at the foot of Prospect Tier, the middle level. He walked to the end of the terrace and looked across to the south side of the gorge. He could see nothing of the top of High Rock and estimated that he had gained only one hundred and fifty feet or so in elevation. Clearly, no one on this terrace or even on Prospect Tier could have had any view of the top of the gorge.

He walked back along the foot of Prospect Tier and rejoined the path to the right, climbing further up the left hand side of the north terraces. There was a stand of trees on his left with a resident population of sheep watching his every move.

He arrived at the start of the terrace at the foot of Heart Leaf Bluff and could see that a fence had been installed along the edge of the terrace. Metal posts had been driven into the ground and wire fencing was strung between each on large steel cables. The fence was also secured in place by retaining cables. Dixon wondered whether it was there to protect tourists below from falling rocks or sheep or perhaps even climbers and decided that it was probably all three.

He walked out to the foot of Dinner Date at the end of the terrace and was surprised to have a clear view of the top of High Rock along the full length of Heart Leaf Bluff. He had not remembered that. Dixon could pick out the line of As the Crow Flies quite clearly, although he found it impossible to estimate the distance between where he stood and the top of the route.

There were a number of small trees all along the top of High Rock. They were just starting to lose their leaves and they appeared to Dixon to be silver birches. They were more than adequate to provide a belay anchor and no doubt they would also have provided cover for anyone tampering with Jake's ropes. It would be a very interesting interview with Carl Harper and his girlfriend.

He took a number of photographs of the top of High Rock and several short sections of video for future reference purposes. He wandered along the foot of Heart Leaf Bluff and found himself trying the handholds at the start of various routes. The rock was overhanging for thirty feet or so and most of the routes were still dry, at least the lower sections. A couple of moves and he was level with the first bolt on a route thirty feet left of Dinner Date. He would have to look up its grade later. Trainers were not ideal footwear and he could feel his leg starting to shake. He turned and jumped, landing heavily in a pile of sheep droppings. He looked up at the cliffs. The memories came flooding back. Routes he could no longer remember the names of, photographs in a box somewhere.

He dropped back down to the Land Rover. There would be just enough time to take Monty for a short walk before Carl Harper arrived. Dixon took Monty into the boulder field beneath the quarried section opposite High Rock and below and to the right of Heart Leaf Bluff. The rock was sharply overhanging and was covered in bolts and chalk marks. He turned to see a red Ford Fiesta pull up behind his Land Rover. He put Monty on his lead and walked back to his car. The occupants of the Ford Fiesta were waiting for him when he arrived.

'Carl Harper?'

'Yes.'

'Detective Inspector Nick Dixon. Thank you very much for coming.'

'Happy to help. It looks as though we'll have plenty of time to talk,' said Harper, holding out his hands to catch the rain.

'It should clear up later. I've just been up onto the terraces and you can see the cloud lifting from the south. You should be OK by lunchtime.'

Dixon bundled Monty into the back of the Land Rover and locked it.

'Would you mind if we walked up to the foot of Dinner Date? I need to get a clear understanding of exactly what you saw at the time.'

'Not at all.'

The three of them walked up to the terrace and out along the fence to the start of Dinner Date. They could see that the cloud was lifting to the southwest.

'Looks like you were right about the weather,' said Harper.

'Yes, you'll be OK for this afternoon, if you choose your route carefully.'

They stood at the foot of Dinner Date where the fence curled round at the end of the terrace. Dixon looked up.

'It's a good route. Did you enjoy it?'

'Yes, very much so. Have you done it?'

'Many years ago. It was an HVS back in the old days.'

Harper laughed. 'When men were men, eh?'

'Something like that.'

Dixon leaned on the fence looking across to High Rock.

'What time did you arrive in the gorge on that day?'

'We got here about five o'clock. I had the day off work and Helen bunked off at lunchtime so we thought we'd get an evening's climbing in.'

'Had you done any routes that day before Dinner Date?'

'No, that was the first one. We came straight up to Heart Leaf Bluff and made a start.'

'Was Jake Fayter already on High Rock when you arrived?'

'Jake Fayter?'

'That was his name.'

'Shit. I didn't know it was him.'

'You knew him?'

'No, but I'd heard of him. He was in the climbing magazines every now and again with new routes and second ascents. Some pretty hairy stuff.'

'Was he on High Rock?'

'Yes. He was just abseiling in when we arrived and we could see him practising a route when we got up to the terrace. What was he working on?'

'A direct finish to Crow. It was going to go at about E7 6c.'

'Shit.'

'What happened then?'

'We got on with Dinner Date. I was leading and Helen was holding the ropes.'

'I was leaning back against the fence post here,' said Helen. She gestured to the last post on the end of the terrace. 'I was watching Carl and had my back to High Rock.'

'A dedicated second,' said Dixon, 'I know it well.'

'I'd never hear the last of it if I wasn't,' replied Helen.

'What happened next?'

'I must have been two thirds of the way up the route. Above the crux, or at least it felt like it. Then there was an almighty shout. I turned to see him falling.'

'What about you, Helen?'

'I heard a shout too and turned to see the fall. It was horrible.'

'Tell me about the shout. Where did it come from?'

'Tourists in the car park, I think.'

'Yes, that's right,' said Helen. 'Some shouts. Some of them were screaming. I could see tourists running down in the car park.'

'Jake Fayter made no sound, then?'

'Come to think of it, no, none at all,' replied Carl.

'I'd have been wailing like I don't know what,' said Helen.

'Had you been watching Jake climbing at all?'

'No, not really. We were concentrating on doing our own route. We'd only got a couple of hours before the light went.'

'Of course,' said Dixon.

Dixon felt the time had come to ask the all important question.

'Did you see anything unusual at the top of High Rock?'

'I didn't,' said Helen. 'The shouts came from below, so when I turned, I looked down to see what was going on. I saw the tourists running and then looked up to see Jake Fayter falling. Thank God I was able to look away just in time.'

'What about you, Carl? You were higher up, weren't you?'

'I heard a shout and looked over my shoulder.'

'Which way?' asked Dixon.

'What do you mean?'

'Which way did you turn?'

'As far as I can remember, I turned to the left and looked over my left shoulder. My weight was on my right leg.'

'Were you in balance at the time?'

'Yes. I'd been placing some gear.'

'So, you heard the shouting, you looked over your left shoulder and what did you see?'

'I saw Jake Fayter falling.'

'What about at the top of High Rock? Think very carefully. This is very important.'

Carl hesitated.

'The trees would've been in full leaf, wouldn't they? What about movement? Did you see any movement in the trees?'

Carl still hesitated. He looked across at Helen. She nodded.

'I get the impression that you have something to tell me, Carl.'

'I saw someone in the trees at the top of High Rock, or at least I think I saw someone.'

'Tell me exactly what you saw.'

'It sounds really crazy but I think I saw a figure moving back through the trees.'

'Male or female?'

'I couldn't tell.'

'Clothing?'

'Dark. Must have been either black or navy blue. Nothing bright.'

'Were they running?'

'Sort of, I think. They were crouched.'

'Did you see where they went?'

'No. I looked down to the shouting below and then I watched Jake fall.'

'How about after that?'

'I looked back to the top of High Rock and the figure was gone.'

'What direction had this person been going in?'

'They were following the line of the trees diagonally to the right.'

Dixon looked across to the top of High Rock and could see a diagonal line of trees ending at the foot of a small outcrop. The exit was to the right of the outcrop, then up and over the back of the gorge. From there the person would have been in cover all the way.

'Did you see this person again? In the car park, perhaps?'

'No.'

'What did you do then?'

'I clipped into the belay at the top and Helen lowered me off. I took all the gear out on the way down and then we dropped back down to the car park to see if we could help.'

'Did you tell anyone what you saw?'

'We gave our names to a police officer who arrived.'

'And no one's been in touch with you since, I suppose?'

'No.'

'Well, they bloody well should have been. I'm sorry about that. Clearly your evidence is vital.'

'I wasn't sure whether to say anything, really. I can't be a hundred per cent sure what I saw, to be honest, and I certainly couldn't identify anyone.'

'I wouldn't expect you to be able to do that. It must be two or three hundred yards across to the top there.'

'I suppose so,' said Carl.

'Let's drop back down to the car park. If you don't mind, I think I'd like to get a statement from you now. You've probably got an hour or so until the rain starts to clear up. What say you we drop down to Costa and get some statements written up?'

'Yes, that's fine,' said Carl.

'You OK with that, Helen?'

'Yes, fine.'

Once back down in the car park they climbed into Dixon's Land Rover. Costa Coffee was only five hundred yards down the gorge but it was still pouring with rain and they had got wet enough up on the terrace. Dixon bought the coffees and they sat in the far corner of Costa, which was practically deserted, giving them a measure of privacy. Dixon hand wrote out a detailed statement from Carl Harper and a short statement from Helen. The essential detail was covered thoroughly. The next step would be for Dixon to persuade DCI Lewis to open a murder investigation.

Dixon dropped Carl and Helen back at their car just before midday. It had stopped raining by then. Dixon wished them a good day's climbing and recommended a route called Morning Glory. Not technically difficult, it took in the full height of the gorge on the south side.

'It's a great day out,' said Dixon. He had done the route with Jake one New Year's Day many years before. It had proved to be a great hangover cure.

Dixon climbed into his Land Rover and looked at his watch. He needed to be home by 2 p.m. to take delivery of a new sofa. Just enough time to have a closer look at the top of High Rock.

Dixon decided that the fastest way to the top of High Rock was to climb. He left his rucksack in the car and put his camera in his pocket. He then walked over to the short slab to the left of the lower car park on the south side of the gorge and looked up. He remembered the slab was very easy. In fact, Jake and he had often used it as a descent route but then that hadn't been in the rain and wearing an old pair of trainers. Nevertheless, he decided to go for it, for old times' sake.

He made short work of the slab itself and then scrambled over the terraces and through the undergrowth to the foot of a route he knew well. Knights Climb was a route that he had done many times, both in ascent and descent. It was graded Difficult, which Dixon reminded himself was the easiest grade of climb, being one step up from a scramble.

Dixon looked up at Knights Climb and could see water pouring down the route. It followed the line of a chimney moving diagonally right up Acid Rock. That would at least mean that he would be able to stay in balance, although he knew that he was going to get soaked to the skin and covered in mud.

The climb was surprisingly dry, but there was a good deal of loose rock in the chimney and more vegetation than he remembered. Knights Climb was not as popular a route as it had once been. He climbed the first section with ease before stepping out onto a steep grass ledge. The chimney continued above him and he could see that the top of the route was now in sunshine. He was starting to enjoy it when he arrived at the top of the chimney to find that a rock fall had removed the last twenty feet or so of the route. This was not part of the plan. The line in front of him was broken and loose and it was obvious from the sediment that it had not been exposed to the elements for very long.

He started to panic. He looked back down the route. Reversing Knights Climb was once something he would have taken in his stride but not now. The only option was to keep going. There was only loose rock and mud in front of him. To his left was the blank wall of Acid Rock. He looked to his right. A heavily vegetated gully offered him an exit and so he took this option. It was his only option. He launched himself into the bushes and arrived at the top a few minutes later. His hands and face were covered in scratches but, all in all, he had enjoyed it.

He followed the top of the cliff to the trees at the top of High Rock. He found the tree that Jake would have used as a belay to abseil over As the Crow Flies. He could see what he thought were marks on the bark left by Jake's tapes and so he took several photographs for his records. Then he followed the line of the trees diagonally and back right to the foot of the small outcrop. He found himself on a path that led round to the right of the outcrop and up over the back of the gorge. Clearly, this had been the escape route.

———

Dixon was back at home just in time to take delivery of his new sofa. When the deliverymen had gone, he opened himself a beer, sat down and reached for his phone.

'DCI Lewis.'

'Nick Dixon, Sir.'

'This had better be good, Dixon. England are playing South Africa and the second half is about to start.'

'I've got a witness on the north side of the gorge who says he saw a figure running away from the top of High Rock at the time Jake fell.'

'Bloody hell.'

'I've got a detailed statement from him, Sir. He will say that he saw a figure crouched and running back from the edge of High Rock.'

'Well done, Nick. Take the rest of the day off, get a good night's sleep and I'll see you in the office at ten sharp tomorrow morning.'

'Thank you, Sir.'

———

'You're a tenacious bugger, Nick.'

'Thank you, Sir.'

'You have your murder investigation. I've cleared it with the chief super. Steve Gorman and Jane Winter can come with you on it, but I think we'd better leave Dave Harding on Magpie at the moment. He can finish that off.'

'A fourth person would be useful.'

'I can let you have Mark Pearce. He's a young detective constable. Very keen and very able, from what I can gather.'

'Do I know him?'

'Probably not. I don't think you've worked with him yet.'

'What about the Weston-super-Mare lot? It's their patch, really.'

'You leave them to me. I suggest you schedule a briefing for 10 a.m. tomorrow. That'll leave you time to make a few calls first. And don't forget the coroner, for heaven's sake.'

'I've already left him a message, Sir.'

'Cheeky sod.'

Dixon spent the afternoon putting all of his papers into one file. He printed off the photographs, photocopied the statements and put them all into a box file. For some reason, even in this digital age, he still felt more comfortable having a paper copy of everything.

He sent emails to the new team, attaching scans of all of the witness statements, the photographs and also the video footage. Hopefully, they would be reasonably familiar with the case before the briefing tomorrow morning. He included the statements from Carl Harper and his girlfriend, Helen, as well as notes of his conversations with Jake's girlfriend, Sarah Heath.

Dixon then rang PC Cole at Cheddar and left a message for him to bring all of the evidence being held there to Bridgwater Police Station first thing in the morning. PC Cole was scheduled to come on duty at 8 a.m. Dixon left him in no doubt that he expected the evidence to arrive at Bridgwater in time for the briefing at 10 a.m.

Dixon suddenly found himself sitting at his desk looking for things to do. He realised that he was putting off going home but knew he could do so no longer. John and Maureen Fayter needed to know what was going on and he would call in to tell them on his way.

Maureen Fayter answered the door.

'Nick, come in. John, it's Nick.' She looked pleased to see him.

John Fayter appeared in the doorway of the sitting room.

'I'm assuming you've got some news for us, Nick?' he said, looking less than pleased to see him.

'I have, but I'm afraid you're not going to like it.'

'We need to hear it all the same, Nick,' said Maureen, 'and we'd rather hear it from you.'

John and Maureen sat side by side on the sofa in the sitting room, holding hands. Dixon sat in the armchair opposite them.

'There's no easy way to say any of this so I'm just come straight out with it, if you'll forgive me.'

'Go ahead,' said John.

'Jake's death is now the subject of a murder investigation.'

Maureen started to cry.

'Keep going,' said John.

'We've got a witness who says that he saw a figure running away from the top of High Rock at precisely the time Jake fell.'

'I bloody knew it,' said John.

'There's no evidence to corroborate this statement yet, and sadly the witness didn't get a clear view of this person, but it does look as though Jake's ropes were interfered with.'

'Why?' said Maureen. 'For God's sake, why?'

'This is where it gets more complicated, I'm afraid.'

'Why?'

'We have to look for possible motives. I'm afraid that I have found two.'

'What?'

'Well, it looks as though Jake was involved in small time drug dealing. He was buying and selling ecstasy tablets for small change, really, but that's one possible motive.'

'We wondered where his money was coming from, didn't we, Maureen?' said John.

Maureen couldn't speak.

'It also looks as though Jake was involved in stealing birds' eggs.'

'Birds' eggs?' said Maureen.

'That's right. Peregrine falcons, to be precise. If you can keep the eggs alive, and get them to the Middle East, they're worth seven thousand pounds each.'

'The trip to Jordan?' asked John.

'He didn't go to Jordan at all, John. He went to Dubai where he sold ten eggs.'

'That's seventy thousand pounds!' said John.

'It is. More than enough motive for murder, I'd have thought. It looks like he was planning to do it again as well because he'd fitted an incubator into the rear seat armrest of his car.'

'We wondered how he afforded to buy that car,' said Maureen.

'I'm afraid it's going to have to be impounded. I'll arrange for it to be collected tomorrow.'

'So, who killed him?' asked John.

'I don't know yet but, in the first instance, I'm looking for his contact. Jake could steal the eggs but he'd have no way of selling them without help. It's that person we need to find.'

'You do what you have to do, Nick,' said John.

Maureen appeared to have gathered her composure.

'Jake bought the Subaru when he got back from Jordan or Dubai or wherever it was he went. So why did he fit the incubator in the armrest?'

'He did it again, Maureen. More eggs and another trip to Dubai. Only something went wrong. I haven't got to the bottom of what yet but he didn't go.'

'He never knew when to quit,' said John.

'Falconry is big business in the Middle East, John.'

Maureen started sobbing again.

'I think I'd better leave you to it,' said Dixon. John Fayter nodded.

'I'll show myself out.'

———⌣———

It had been an early start. Dawn and dusk had always been the best times to catch pike but these days it was a rare occasion when he got out of bed much before 9 a.m. at the weekend. This morning his alarm had gone off at 5 a.m. It was still dark. He had made a Thermos flask of coffee and had stopped at the petrol station to get some sandwiches and chocolate. He had put his fishing tackle in the car the night before and had arrived at Gold Corner Pumping Station before sunrise.

He parked in the muddy car park opposite the farm and walked through the wooden five bar gates. He followed the muddy farm track over Powder Sluice on the River Cripps and then climbed over the five bar gate into the field. He was now behind the farm and the pumping station and walking along the South Drain, his favourite pike fishing venue.

He followed the north bank for about eight hundred yards towards the metal bridge that took the farm track over the drain. There was a slight bend at this point with sluices bringing small streams into the drain on either side, creating small bays. Ideal features for pike. This had always been a favourite spot.

He put up his large umbrella to get some shelter from the wind and tackled up by the light of his head torch. By sunrise, he was ready to start. He was fishing two rods and cast one into the bay opposite and the other along the nearside bank. Each had a small mackerel on the hook that he hoped would take the fancy of any pike roving along either the far or the near bank.

The wind had dropped and in the morning light he could see cows in the fields behind him and opposite grazing gently on the wet grass. He could hear the buzz of the electricity pylons and spotted several vapour trails glowing red in the morning sun. A buzzard was wheeling overhead.

By mid-afternoon he had caught three good sized pike, the largest weighing in at just over seventeen pounds. It was turning out to be a good day.

He could see a figure walking along the bank towards him. He was wearing dark trousers and a blue coat. It would be the Environment Agency bailiff coming to check his licence. A regular occurrence and nothing to worry about. He reached into his pocket to check that his licence was in his wallet.

'May I see your licence, Sir?'

He turned to find himself looking straight into the barrel of a gun. He didn't have time to look up. He saw the trigger finger twitch. He felt a sharp pain in his right eye and then darkness began to take him. He felt numb. Suddenly he was falling forward. He heard a splash. He could not breathe but there was no panic and no pain. He felt cold.

Chapter Eight

Dixon started the briefing at 10 a.m. He noticed DCI Lewis sitting at the back of the room, as usual. Steve Gorman and Jane Winter were leaning on the desks nearest the whiteboard. DC Mark Pearce was sitting at the desk Gorman was leaning on. Pearce was of medium build. He had short dark hair and wore a jacket and tie. He clearly took pride in his appearance and Dixon thought that if he turned out to be half as efficient as he looked then he would be an asset to the investigation.

'Did everyone get the emails I sent yesterday morning?'

All agreed that they had.

'Good, so you have a reasonable grasp of where we are. Let's deal with the admin first. Jane, can you rustle up a lorry to fetch Jake's car? It's at his parents' place in Braithwaite Place, Burnham-on-Sea.'

'Yes, Sir.'

'PC Cole has brought over the evidence from Cheddar. I've signed for it. Mark, can you get it booked in, please? There's a telescopic golf ball retriever in my office too.'

'Yes, Sir.'

'I've got his laptop in the drawer of my desk. We need to get it over to High Tech. And don't forget his iPhone. Jane?'

'No problem. Any specific instructions?'

'We'll come onto that in a minute. Right, let's have a look at the players themselves.'

Dixon turned to the whiteboard and pointed to the photo of Jake Fayter.

'This is Jake Fayter. The victim.'

Jake was smiling at the camera. His blonde hair was tied back in a ponytail. He wore a white Bruce Springsteen T-shirt and there was a sea cliff visible in the background. Probably Pembroke, Dixon thought. Jake was in his element.

'We know that he was supplying ecstasy and he was the prime suspect for the supply of the fatal dose of PMA to Jenna Williams. Steve, perhaps you can fill us in on that?'

'We had a clear statement from Conrad Benton with a positive ID of Fayter and the Williams girl in an alley outside Rococo's just before she was found dead. It was fairly straightforward, to be honest, although Benton is not the most reliable of witnesses, perhaps.'

'Why the delay in arresting Fayter?' asked Dixon.

'We were looking for other evidence to corroborate Benton's statement and I didn't want to let Fayter know we were onto him. Simple as that, really.'

'Well, we can come back to that later.'

'You'd have done it differently, I suppose?'

'Seeing as you have asked, Steve, yes I would. I'd have brought him straight in and let him know I was onto him. Let him sweat. But it was your investigation, your decision and you made it.'

'I did.'

Dixon ignored him.

'What I'm not clear about is whether Fayter knew he was pushing PMA on the night in question.'

'We never interviewed him so I don't know. Is it relevant?' replied Gorman.

'Probably not, but I'm pretty sure it was Benton who supplied it to him. Jane, dig out everything we have on Benton, will you? When this is over I'm going to be crawling in and out of every one of that tosser's orifices until his eyes bulge.'

'It'll be a pleasure, Sir,' said Jane.

'We know Jake was also stealing peregrine falcon eggs and selling them in the Middle East. His partner in this enterprise was Dan Hunter.' Dixon stuck a photograph of Hunter on the whiteboard and drew an arrow between the two.

'Is there any evidence that Hunter was also involved in the dealing?' asked Jane.

'No. But the birds' eggs are where the real money is. We need to bring Hunter in straight away. I met him at Jake's funeral on Friday and he's agreed to help in any way he can. We'll see what that means. At the very least, he's looking at two years for offences under the Wildlife and Countryside Act, but he doesn't know that we know about that yet and I'd like to keep it that way until I interview him.'

'Two years?'

'Yes, Mark. It's a serious business. Thirty months someone got at Warwick Crown Court only a couple of years ago.'

'Shit.'

'I'm convinced that Hunter holds the key to Jake's murder. Someone was setting up these deals and it's that person we need to find. Hunter can lead us to him.'

'What went wrong with the second deal, Sir?' asked Jane.

'I don't know yet. That's another question for Hunter. Jake collected the eggs, possibly with Hunter, and then didn't go to Dubai to see it through. We need access to Jake's bank accounts. See if he got his cut of the second deal. Mark?'

'I'll see to it, Sir.'

'Let's get Hunter in straight away. Steve, can you make that your priority? I'll conduct the interview.'

'OK.'

'We'll need to have a look at his computer and phone too. Mark, can you give him a hand with that?'

'Will do, Sir.'

'Which brings me back to Jake's computer, Jane. We need the High Tech Unit to have a look at it for any evidence of contact with person or persons unknown. Tell them to check his Facebook account and anything like that.'

'Right, Sir.'

'Email will be too obvious, I think. It'll be Facebook messaging or something like that. Skype, perhaps. Tell them to check the FaceTime on his iPhone too.'

'Will do, Sir.'

'Right, that leaves you and me, Jane. We need to get a formal statement from Jake's girlfriend, Sarah Heath.'

He turned to the whiteboard and stuck a photograph of Sarah Heath next to Jake's. He drew an arrow between the two.

'Who is that, Sir?' asked Pearce.

'Sarah Heath. Jake's girlfriend.'

'No, it's not.'

'What?' Dixon's voice was an octave higher.

'Well, she may be Jake's girlfriend and she may be called Sarah Heath, but she's also Jenna Williams' sister.'

Dixon looked at Mark Pearce then at the photograph of Sarah on the whiteboard. He looked back to Pearce. He saw Lewis sit up sharply at the back of the room.

'Explain.'

'She was with Jenna's mother when she came to identify the body.'

'Steve?'

'I wasn't there, Sir.'

'There's no mention of this in the file.'

'We never made the connection,' said Gorman. 'We were watching Fayter, of course, but never saw them together.'

'Were you involved in that, Mark?'

'Yes, but I never saw him with his girlfriend.'

'Maybe she didn't know,' said Jane.

'Maybe she killed him,' said Gorman.

'Well, we'll soon find out. Let's get cracking. Meet back here at 5 p.m. Jane, we'll leave in twenty minutes.'

Dixon went back to his office. He sat down and started to count to ten. He had reached six when the door opened and DCI Lewis came in.

'The girlfriend it is, then?'

'I doubt it, Sir. I don't think she knew.'

'The mother, then?'

'How would she have known Jake was dealing drugs?'

'Sarah could have told her?'

'Unlikely. It's not the sort of thing you'd admit to your mother, is it?'

'No, I suppose not.'

'Sarah certainly knew Jake was selling ecstasy round the clubs but that's it, I think. She may have put two and two together, of course, but she'd want firm evidence before killing him over it, surely?'

'He may have admitted it to her?'

'True.'

'Just don't rule it out, Nick. We may be looking at a simple revenge killing and unrelated wildlife offences.'

'That'd be too easy, Sir.'

Dixon tried to sound confident but there was a nagging doubt in his mind. Something was telling him that Sarah had known. Possibly. He hoped it would come to him before they brought her in for interview.

⌣

Steve Gorman could just about make out the figure of Mark Pearce huddled on the doorstep of number 12 Wells Close, Burnham-on-Sea. His windscreen wipers were working at full speed but that still only afforded him brief glimpses of Pearce through the torrential rain. He had been listening to the phone in on Radio 5 Live. It was coming to an end and he reached down to switch it off when there was a loud tapping at the car window. He pressed the button just long enough to wind the window down an inch.

'There's no one in.'

'Try the neighbours.'

Gorman wound the window back up as quickly as he could and watched Pearce run across the lawn to the property immediately adjacent to 12 Wells Close. It was one of the advantages of his rank. He had done plenty of running about in the rain as a junior constable and now it was someone else's turn.

He looked along the line of six modern red brick semi-detached properties, built in three pairs in the middle of Wells Close. Number 12 was Dan Hunter's house. Each property had a built in garage and, Gorman thought, probably three bedrooms. The lawn was neat and tidy and there were rows of flowerpots outside the front door and along the path at the side. Dan Hunter definitely needed to get out more.

Mark Pearce turned to the car and gave an exaggerated shrug of the shoulders. Gorman pointed to the next property along and watched as Pearce turned and walked across the lawn. He was making no effort to shield himself from the rain now and looked soaked through.

Gorman was surprised to see Pearce get a response at number 16. He had expected most people to be out. He could see Pearce produce his warrant card. The conversation appeared to be quite animated, at least as far as Mark Pearce was concerned, and Gorman guessed that the elderly woman to whom he was talking was deaf. After a few minutes, Pearce ran back across to the car and jumped into the passenger seat.

'Pissing down it is.'

'I can see that.'

'I'm bloody soaked now.'

Pearce reached inside his jacket pocket and produced his notebook. He began making notes as he spoke.

'Mrs Morton at number 16 Wells Close. Totally deaf. I thought for a minute she was going to invite me in, but no luck. It was difficult enough having a conversation with her without the rain hammering on the porch roof. She told me that the people from number 14 are on holiday. She last saw Dan Hunter on Saturday afternoon. He was packing his fishing tackle into his car.'

'And she's not seen him since then?'

'No. But then she wouldn't have expected to. If he'd gone fishing on the Sunday he'd have got back after dark. Not only that, but he's a postman and would've been up and away to work long before she got up on Monday morning.'

'What about his car?'

'Mrs Morton says that it would usually be parked in the drive. He'd have driven to work on a day like this though, surely?'

'The sorting offices are just around the corner in Dunstan Road,' said Gorman.

'That's right. Mrs Morton said that he usually cycles to work.'

'Did she say what type of car he's got?'

'Green and an estate car. That's all she knows.'

'OK, let's try the sorting office.'

It took less than two minutes to drive the short distance to Dunstan Road. Another cul-de-sac. The Royal Mail sorting office was at the far end, given away by the high fencing and line of red vans parked outside.

'A few too many cul-de-sacs in this man's life for my liking,' said Pearce.

'What?'

'He lives in a cul-de-sac and works in a cul-de-sac. Bit of a dead end life, wouldn't you say?'

'Is that supposed to be funny?'

'No, Sarge. It just struck me as odd, that's all.'

They parked in the car park outside the main reception and walked into the front office. The reception consisted of a counter with a bell on it and a small waiting area. Gorman rang the bell and they waited. A few moments later, a postman appeared behind the counter.

'How can I help?'

Gorman and Pearce both produced their warrant cards. 'We were looking for the manager.'

'She's not in today. I'll get the assistant manager,' said the postman, turning to leave the room.

'What's his name?' asked Pearce.

'Linda Dickinson.'

Gorman glared at Pearce, who shrugged his shoulders in reply.

Linda Dickinson checked their warrant cards and then showed them through to her office. She was in her late forties with bleached shoulder length hair and wore a Royal Mail uniform.

'Please sit down. I'm the assistant manager. What can I do for you?'

'We're looking for Dan Hunter,' said Gorman.

'Is he in trouble?'

'No, but we're hoping that he may be able to assist with an ongoing enquiry,' explained Gorman.

'Well, the short answer to your question is that we haven't seen him since he finished work on Saturday. He should have been here today but didn't turn up. We've tried ringing him at home and on his mobile. No answer. I finish work in a couple of hours and was going to knock on his door on my way home.'

'We've just been there and there's no one in,' said Gorman.

'I wonder what's happened to him then?' asked Linda. 'He's usually very good at ringing in if he's sick or something.'

'Did he mention anything to anybody on Saturday?'

'Not as far as I know. It was just a perfectly normal Saturday shift.'

'What delivery route does he cover?' asked Pearce.

'He's been doing the rural deliveries recently. Small hamlets, outlying cottages, farms, that sort of thing. He likes being out and about in the van.'

'Did he mention the death of his climbing partner, Jake Fayter?' asked Gorman.

'He mentioned it once or twice. I knew he was upset by it and he took time off to go to the funeral, of course. Is this anything to do with that?'

'We really can't say, I'm afraid,' replied Gorman.

'His neighbour said he might have gone fishing on Sunday?' asked Pearce.

'Yes, that's possible,' replied Linda. 'Climbing in the summer and fishing in the winter, I think it was.'

'Did you know him well?' asked Gorman.

'As well as you know anyone you've worked with seventeen years.'

'Did he have any friends he worked with?'

'Yes, a couple. Tim was probably his best friend. Tim Keenan.'

'Can we speak to him?' asked Gorman.

'He's out on deliveries at the moment but he'll be back in a couple of hours.'

Gorman produced his calling card and handed it to Linda Dickinson.

'Could you ask Mr Keenan to call me on my mobile as soon as he gets back? We won't be far away and can pop straight over to have a word with him.'

'Yes, of course,' replied Linda.

'Thank you very much, you've been very helpful. Can we leave our car here?'

'Certainly.'

Gorman and Pearce walked along Dunstan Road towards the town centre.

'Where are we going?' asked Pearce.

'Breakfast.'

'We'll take your car if we may, Jane. I don't think Miss Heath is going to want Monty breathing down her neck on the way back.'

'You never know, she may be a dog person.'

Dixon smiled.

They drove in silence out through Bridgwater and north on the M5 towards Burnham-on-Sea. Torrential rain made the driving conditions difficult. Conversation was all but impossible with the noise of the rain and Jane's windscreen wipers at full speed. Once off the motorway, Dixon felt able to speak.

'You can do the talking, I think. I'll step in and ruffle her feathers when I think the time is right.'

'OK.'

'Tell me something, Jane.'

'What, Sir?'

'Is there some six foot gorilla who would leap on me from a great height if I asked you out to dinner?'

'Dinner?'

'Yes, dinner.'

'On a date, you mean?'

'Well, that depends.'

'What on?'

'Your answer. If it's a yes, then it's a date. If it's no, then of course it wasn't a date. You just got your wires crossed.'

'Hedging your bets, then?'

'Like any good bookmaker . . .'

'The answer to your question is no, there is no six foot gorilla, but I didn't think that relationships with senior officers were the done thing?'

'I'm hardly the chief constable. When you pass your sergeant's exams, I'll only be one rank above you.'

'I suppose so.'

'I tell you what. Here's the deal. As soon as I'm appointed chief constable, I'll dump you straight away. How's that?'

'Dinner it is, then,' said Jane, smiling, 'on one condition.'

'Sounds ominous.'

'You tell me about this medal.'

'Over dinner.'

'Done.'

Jane turned right off Berrow Road into The Grove.

'Back to the business in hand. Usual drill when we pick her up, arrest her if needs be and then take her through the whole story from the top in interview. Press her on the argument outside the Vic the night before Jake died too. I think that's our man. I'll step in as and when.'

'She's going to love you.'

Sarah Heath answered the door. She did not look pleased to see them.

'What the fuck is it now?'

'I am Detective Constable Jane Winter. I believe you know Detective Inspector Nick Dixon, Sarah?'

'Yes, and I've told him everything I know.'

'I have to inform you that the death of Jake Fayter is now the subject of a murder investigation and we need a for—'

'Murder investigation?'

'Yes. We have reason to believe that his climbing ropes were tampered with.'

'Oh fuck.'

Sarah started crying.

'We need you to accompany us to Bridgwater Police Station, please, and—'

'I told you everything I know.'

'We believe that there may be further matters with which you can assist us,' said Jane, 'and I must insist that you accompany us to Bridgwater Police Station.'

'And what if I tell you to fuck off?'

'Then I'd have to arrest you, which will make for an uncomfortable ride to the police station in handcuffs and a lot of extra paperwork.'

Sarah glared at Dixon. 'Is this for real?'

'It is,' said Dixon.

'But I've told you the truth.'

'The truth, the whole truth and nothing but the truth . . .'

'What the hell is that supposed to mean?'

'You've told me the truth,' said Dixon. 'I have no doubt about that. Nothing but the truth? Probably. But have you told me the whole truth? I don't think so.'

'What do I tell work?'

'You could try telling them the truth too,' replied Dixon. He nodded to Jane to take over.

'Come on Sarah, get your coat.'

'How long is this going to take?'

'That depends on you.'

The drive to Bridgwater Police Station was uneventful and silent. Sarah Heath was booked in, cautioned and offered the opportunity of legal representation. She declined a solicitor on the grounds that she had nothing to hide. After the usual introductions and a reminder that she was under caution, the interview began just before 11 a.m.

Dixon sat in silence while Jane took a formal statement from Sarah Heath. The interview was tape recorded and, as planned, covered all of the information already given by Sarah. Jane went through it all again in minute detail, covering where Sarah lived and worked, her relationship with Jake, how and when they met, Jake's drug dealing and known associates, as well as his rock climbing activities and birds' egg collecting. As instructed, Jane questioned Sarah closely on the argument outside the Vic but got nothing new.

During the course of the interview, Sarah's emotions ranged from anger, irritation and frustration through to tears and sadness, depending upon the line of questioning at the time. Dixon felt sure that her emotional response in each instance was genuine and, whilst no new information emerged, he was impressed with Jane's meticulous approach.

After a little over two hours of questioning, the interview appeared to be drawing to a natural conclusion. Jane looked at Dixon, who gave an almost imperceptible nod.

'Let's go back to Jake's drug dealing,' said Jane.

'For fuck's sake, we've been through that already.'

'We'll go through it one more time if we may. Which night-clubs did Jake frequent in Bridgwater?'

'Rococo's and the Paradise. They're the only two. I've already told you.'

Dixon could see that Sarah was becoming angry. He leaned across the table and spoke slowly and quietly.

'When did you find out that Jake killed your sister?'

Sarah sat back in her chair. Tears began to stream down her cheeks. She looked up at the ceiling and then back to Dixon. She opened her mouth to speak but instead began sobbing. Dixon waited.

'I . . .' the words were lost in tears.

'I believe what you've told me so far, so please don't lie to me now.'

Sarah fixed Dixon in the gaze of her bloodshot eyes.

'I thought it a bit odd that you bagged up his belongings and dumped them at his parents' house so soon after he died,' said Dixon.

Sarah sat up in her chair and wiped away the tears with the palms of her hands.

'I found out the day after he died.'

'On the Saturday?' Dixon continued the questioning.

'Yes.'

'Why didn't you mention this before?'

'Because I knew what you'd think. You'd think I killed him.'

'I don't, as it happens, but then I've been wrong before.'

'I didn't kill him.'

'I need to know how you found out about Jenna.'

'I was working Friday night as usual and Jake wasn't in when I got home about midnight. I thought he was probably out in either Bridgwater or Weston so I went to bed.'

'Go on.'

'He still wasn't back when I woke up in the morning so I tried his mobile and got no reply. Then his father rang me. I was in a bit of a state so I told work I wouldn't be in and went to see my mum.'

'OK, so that's how you found out about Jake's death. How did you find out he supplied the drugs to Jenna?'

'I can't tell you that.'

'Why not?'

'Because you'll think they killed Jake.'

'So this person knew before Jake died that he supplied the drugs to Jenna?'

'I suppose so.'

'I think we need to have a word with your mother then, don't we?'

'She didn't kill him.' Sarah was now sobbing uncontrollably.

'Who told her?'

'I don't know, a policeman, I think.'

'And she knew before Jake died that he was suspected of supplying the drugs that killed her youngest daughter. Is that right, Sarah?'

'Yes, but she didn't kill him.'

'Where will we find your mum?'

'I don't know. She's probably still at work.'

'Where is that?'

'The sorting office in Burnham-on-Sea. She's the manager.'

Steve Gorman was sitting on the seafront with Mark Pearce, enjoying an ice cream, when his phone rang.

'Steve Gorman.'

'Steve, it's Nick Dixon.'

'Yes, Sir.' Gorman turned to Pearce and raised his eyebrows.

'Have you found Hunter?'

'No, Sir. He's not at work or at home. We're just waiting for a work colleague to get back so we can have a word with him.'

'What about neighbours?'

'A Mrs Morton at number 16 Wells Close says that she saw him getting his fishing tackle ready on Saturday afternoon, but she's not seen him since. The assistant manager at the sorting office says that he didn't turn up for work this morning either.'

'Sorting office?'

'Yes, Sir. Hunter is a postman.'

'Did you see the manager?'

'No, she's not in today. We saw the assistant manager, Linda Dickinson.'

'The manager, Steve, is Tina Williams. Jenna Williams' mother.'

'Oh, shit.'

'How much longer is this work colleague likely to be?'

'I'm expecting a call any moment now.'

'OK, get a statement from him. Ask him if he knows where Hunter might have gone fishing and, if not, what type of fishing he did.'

'Type of fishing?'

'Yes, that will tell us where he might have gone. Then I need you to get over to 17 Bason Bridge Lane, East Huntspill, and pick up Tina Williams.'

'Right.'

'According to her daughter, she knew that Jake had supplied the drugs to Jenna but, at the moment, she is just helping us with our enquiries. Right?'

'Yes, Sir, we'll be as quick as we can.'

Dixon stood in front of the whiteboard with DCI Lewis, having spotted him coming a fraction too late to make good his escape.

'Any developments, Nick?'

'I've interviewed Sarah Heath, who says that she found out after Jake died that he had supplied the drugs to her sister.'

'Why didn't she mention it before?'

'So we didn't think that she killed Jake, apparently, but the reality is that she was probably protecting the person who told her.'

'And who was that?'

'Her mother.'

'Her mother?'

'Yes. Imagine knowing that your eldest daughter's boyfriend supplied the drugs that killed your youngest daughter.'

'Motive enough for murder, surely?'

'Possibly.'

'Anything else?'

'Dan Hunter has gone missing, or at least Steve Gorman can't find him.'

'Gorman couldn't find his own backside with both hands.'

'I'll take your word for that, Sir. The interesting point, though, is that Hunter is a postman based at the sorting office in Burnham-on-Sea where Tina Williams, Jenna Williams' mother, is the manager.'

'Bloody hell.'

'The obvious conclusion is that Tina Williams killed Jake and possibly also Dan Hunter to shut him up,' said Dixon. 'But it's just too obvious.'

'Or Hunter killed Jake at Tina's bidding?'

'Both are possible, Sir, but I still think we're barking up the wrong tree.'

'What are you doing about it?'

'I've got Jake's girlfriend, Sarah, in the cells. Gorman has picked up Tina Williams and should be here in about twenty minutes, I'm told.'

'Good. Let me know how you get on.'

The interview with Tina Williams began just after 4 p.m. She had been cautioned on arrival at Bridgwater Police Station and had exercised her right to legal representation. This had resulted in a delay of nearly an hour while they waited for a police station accredited solicitor. Dixon used the opportunity to take Monty for a walk. He had always regarded the accreditation process for solicitors to be something of nonsense because most of them were clerks without a qualification to their name. Having said that, he hoped that the possibility of a murder charge might bring out someone who knew what they were doing.

Tina Williams was in her mid-fifties with short dark hair and greying roots. She was wearing jeans and a knitted pullover. After the usual introductions for the tape and a reminder that she was still under caution, Dixon began.

'We are investigating the murder of Jake Fayter, Tina. Sarah's boyfriend.'

'I know.'

'How well did you know Jake?'

'Not that well. He'd only been going out with Sarah for about a year.'

'How often did you see him?'

'Not that often. He was always away climbing or, at least, that was what Sarah told me.'

'Did you like him?'

'He was nice enough but I didn't like what he was doing.'

'Dealing drugs?'

'Yes.'

'You knew he was dealing drugs?'

'Yes. Sarah told me.'

'Why would she tell you that? It's hardly the sort of thing that you'd admit to your mother, that your boyfriend is a drug dealer, is it?'

'I couldn't understand where he got his money from but I eventually got it out of her. I begged her to leave him but she wouldn't.'

'When did you find out that it was Jake who'd supplied the drugs to Jenna?'

Tina looked across at her solicitor who smiled reassuringly and nodded. She began to cry.

'I really don't want to upset you unnecessarily, Tina, but it's important that we understand when you found out that Jake may have supplied the drugs to your daughter. We're investigating a murder and I'm sure you would agree that it gives you a powerful motive for wanting Jake dead.'

'I didn't kill him.'

'When did you find out about Jake?'

'About a week after Jenna died. It was before her funeral. He came to it, the little shit, crying buckets. How I didn't kill him then I'll never know.'

Dixon glanced across at Jane Winter, who raised her eyebrows. They could see Tina's solicitor writing furiously in his notebook.

'Who told you?'

'A policeman. The one investigating the case.'

'What was his name?'

'I can't remember. It was the same policeman who brought me here.'

'What did he tell you?'

'He told me that they had a suspect and were trying to get more evidence against him. He said he was a rock climber. I mean, who else could it have been?'

'He didn't mention Jake Fayter by name?'

'No.'

'Tell me about Dan Hunter.'

'What do you want to know? He works with me at the sorting office and has done for about seventeen years.'

'He was Jake's climbing partner?'

'Yes. Dan was interested in climbing so I put them in touch. That was before I knew what Jake was up to.'

'Did they go climbing often?'

'From what I can gather but I didn't know Dan that well, to be honest. He's a postman and I'm the depot manager.'

'Were you aware that Dan didn't turn up for work today?'

'No, I've had the day off. Linda, my assistant, would've sorted that out.'

Dixon paused.

'Are you glad that Jake is dead?'

Tina's solicitor looked up.

'My client doesn't have to answer that question.'

'It's all right,' said Tina. 'No, I am not glad he is dead. It doesn't bring my daughter back, does it? I'm glad that he's out of Sarah's life but not that he's dead.'

Dixon brought the interview to a close. It had been short but it had confirmed what he already knew. Neither Tina Williams nor Sarah Heath had killed Jake. He turned to Jane Winter.

'Release them, Jane. Ask the desk sergeant to lay on a car to take them home.'

'Lewis will go mad!'

'This isn't about the drugs, and you and I both know it. This is about the birds' eggs. I'll stake my job on it.'

'I think you just did, Sir.'

Dixon was sitting in his office ten minutes later when the door flew open and Steve Gorman barged in.

'You let them go. What the hell did you do that for?'

'Shut the door.' Dixon spoke calmly and quietly. Gorman shut the door. Dixon gestured to the chair in front of his desk.

'Sit down.'

Gorman sat down. Dixon waited until he did so and then stood up.

'First things first, Steve. If you barge into my office and speak to me like that again, you and I are going to fall out big time.'

Gorman opened his mouth to reply but Dixon dismissed it with a wave of his hand.

'Secondly, it is my investigation, and if I choose to release a suspect or suspects then that is my decision and mine alone. Clear?'

'Yes, Sir.'

'You should also be aware that Tina Williams has confirmed in interview that you gave her sufficient information to identify Jake as the suspect in the death of her daughter.'

'I didn't tell her anything.'

'You told her that the suspect was a rock climber and that was enough, apparently.'

'Oh, shit.'

'Thanks to you, she knew before Jenna's funeral that Jake was the prime suspect.'

'But she didn't kill him.'

'No, I don't think she did. Anyway, this is going to be out of my hands now, I'm afraid.'

'Yes, Sir.'

'Now, let's try and get this investigation back on track. Get onto DVLA and get a detailed description of Hunter's car. I also need the statements that you took this morning.'

'Yes, Sir.' Gorman got up to leave Dixon's office.

'Make sure everyone is available for a short meeting at six o'clock, will you?'

'Yes, Sir.'

———————

'Not a good day, all in all,' said Dixon. Mercifully, DCI Lewis was not listening in.

'What progress on Hunter's car, Steve?'

'It's a green VW Passat estate, Sir. 2005, so it's the old shape. Registration number FYY 922,' said Gorman.

'Must be a personalised number plate or something, I suppose?'

'Yes, Sir.'

'We need to find Hunter tomorrow.' Dixon addressed Steve Gorman and DC Mark Pearce. 'I want you two sat outside his house first thing in the morning and, if he hasn't turned up by lunchtime, we'll get a warrant and go in.'

'Is stealing birds' eggs an arrestable offence, Sir?' asked Mark Pearce.

'Yes it is. We also need to be looking for Hunter's car. We know he hasn't been seen since he went fishing, assuming, of course, that he actually went fishing. We know from the statement from Tim Keenan that Hunter used to go pike fishing this time of year, so we need to get all of the car parks along the King's Sedgemoor Drain and also Gold Corner Pumping Station checked for starters. Mark, can you get the local boys onto that in the morning?'

'Yes, Sir.'

'Any news on the bank statements?'

'I've got Fayter's and there's a transfer in from a Swiss account and then the payment out to the Subaru garage. Not much else. I'm still waiting for Dan Hunter's to arrive,' replied Mark Pearce.

'Jane, can you chase up the High Tech Unit, please? We still haven't had their report on Jake's laptop and iPhone.'

'I'll get onto that first thing in the morning, Sir.'

'OK. Well, that's enough for today. I can feel a beer coming on, I think.'

Chapter Nine

Dixon spent the morning reviewing the enhanced photographs and video footage of Jake taken by the tourists in the gorge. He could see Jake fighting the shakes until he could hang on no longer. He felt mixed emotions now, his sadness tempered by the knowledge that Jake had been dealing drugs and stealing birds' eggs, but he remained grateful that the cameraman had turned away at the finish. He learned nothing new from the footage, nor did he from Jake's bank statements. Apart from the money arriving from Switzerland and the payment to the Subaru garage, there was very little activity, confirming, perhaps, that Jake lived hand to mouth on cash.

Dixon knew that he needed to track down the dealer with the contacts in Dubai, and the seventy thousand pounds from the sale of the second batch of eggs. It was looking increasingly unlikely that Dan Hunter would be able to shed any light on this. Lunchtime had come and gone with still no sign of him and a search warrant was now being executed at 12 Wells Close, Burnham-on-Sea. Hopefully, that would turn up something useful.

Just after 3 p.m. there was a knock on his office door. It was Jane Winter.

'Jane, any news on Hunter's bank statements?'

'Not yet, Sir, but we have found his car.'

'Where is it?'

'Gold Corner Pumping Station.'

'I told them to look there this morning, for heaven's sake.'

'And there's some abandoned fishing tackle out on the . . . er . . . South Drain, is it?'

'Yes it is. Ring Steve Gorman and let him know. Then get your wellies.'

Dixon turned right into the narrow country lane on the sharp bend before he reached East Huntspill. He followed the single track lane carefully. He knew from experience that there were deep drainage ditches either side and the low evening sun was directly in his eyes as he headed towards Gold Corner Pumping Station. Some relief from the glare was offered by the occasional bush or tree but the Somerset Levels were a bleak and open place at the best of times, offering little in the way of shade or shelter.

He arrived at Gold Corner Pumping Station and pulled into the car park to be met by PC Stevens, who had made the call. Dixon was assured that scenes of crime officers were on their way and that a flatbed lorry had also been summoned to recover Hunter's car.

'What about divers?'

'Coming from Bristol, Sir. It's likely to be dark before they get here.'

'Better tell 'em to bring their torches, then.'

'Yes, Sir.'

'Any CCTV on the pumping station?' Dixon pointed to the large brick and glass building at the junction of the South Drain and the River Huntspill.

'I'll check, Sir.'

Dixon went to the back of his Land Rover and put on his wellington boots. Jane did the same.

'Which side of the Drain is it, Constable?'

'That side, Sir,' said Stevens, gesturing to the north. 'Do you know the way?'

'I do, yes, thank you.'

Dixon crossed the road and went through the wooden five bar gate. Jane followed. They took the muddy farm track around to the right, over the River Cripps and went into the field adjacent to the South Drain. They walked along the north bank of the South Drain in the short section that ran behind the farm and the pumping station. Dixon could see fishing tackle hanging in the trees. They followed the bank around to the left and out onto the main section of the drain.

The South Drain was part of the original drainage system that created the Somerset Levels. It was thirty yards wide and twelve to fifteen feet deep. The Environment Agency had announced some time ago their intention to dredge it along its full length to create a deeper channel and so the North Somerset Angling Association had given up their licence to fish it. There had been no maintenance of the banks in recent years as a result and they had become overgrown. Nevertheless, it still held a good head of fish and was a popular venue, particularly now that no angling club licence was required.

In the distance, Dixon could see several figures standing on the north bank. He guessed that this was where Dan Hunter had been fishing and set off along the bank to get there as quickly as possible. Jane followed, struggling in the mud.

Dixon arrived at the fishing umbrella to see three uniformed police officers and the farmer, Michael Wilkins. Dan Hunter had chosen his spot carefully. His seat was sheltered by the bank rising up on either side, with the umbrella acting as a roof of sorts. There were also small bushes on either side offering more cover.

'No sign of Hunter, I suppose?'

'No, Sir.'

'Have you looked?'

'We've checked in the immediate vicinity.'

'What about footprints?'

One of the police constables gestured towards the cows.

'They've been all over the place, Sir.'

'They're a bit inquisitive, I'm afraid,' said Mr Wilkins.

'You'll be the farmer?' asked Dixon.

'Yes.'

'Do you know how long this stuff has been here?'

'Not really. It wasn't here when I came out on Saturday but I've not been out here since then. Not till today.'

'What about the car in the car park?'

'I don't take much notice of them. They come and go and there's a big hedge between my house and the car park anyways.'

It was a typical fishing scene, although the fisherman himself was missing. There was a reclining chair under a large green umbrella with a box of fishing tackle next to it and a landing net lying in the grass. Dixon noticed an area of what looked like blood spattered on the underside of the umbrella.

He noticed that there were two sets of rod rests but only one fishing rod. He produced a pair of disposable rubber gloves from his pocket and put them on. He reached down, picked up the fishing rod and reeled it in. There was nothing on the line and the bait had gone. He placed the hook in the first eye on the rod nearest the reel, wound the line tight and replaced the rod on the rests. Then he picked up a set of forceps and the landing net and set off along the bank towards the footbridge. Jane followed.

'What are we looking for, Sir?'

'The other fishing rod.'

'Why?'

'You'll see.'

Fifty yards further along the bank, they could see the fishing rod floating on the edge of a patch of lily pads. Dixon was able to reach it with the landing net and draw it in close to the bank. He reached down, picked it up and wound the line in. Almost immediately the rod arched over. There was a fish on the end. Dixon had the fish in the landing net within a couple of minutes.

'You've done this before, Sir,' said Jane.

'Many years ago.'

'Is there no end to your talents?'

'No, there isn't,' replied Dixon, smiling.

He flipped the pike onto its back in the long grass, placed his fingers under the gill rake at the front of the jaw and then opened the fish's mouth. He reached in with the forceps, unhooked it and then held it gently in the water until it swam away. It took no more than sixty seconds.

'Well done, Sir.'

'She'll live to fight another day.'

'She?' asked Jane.

'You can tell by the size. Males don't get that big.'

'There's a joke in there somewhere.'

They walked back to the umbrella to find scenes of crime officers arriving with PC Stevens.

'The divers will be here in about twenty minutes, Sir,' said Stevens. 'And there's no CCTV on the pumping station, unfortunately.'

'Thank you, Constable.'

Dixon turned to the scenes of crime officers.

'There's blood spatter on the inside of the umbrella that you'll need to take a close look at. You may get something from the footprints hereabouts although I'm told that the cows have been wandering about everywhere. I'm guessing our man is in the water.'

The senior scenes of crime officer was a tall balding man with a moustache who Dixon had encountered before. His name was

Watson, and whilst Dixon did not find him an altogether personable man, he was at least efficient.

'How long has is it been, do we know?' asked Watson.

'Not with any degree of certainty,' replied Dixon. 'The farmer says that there was nobody here on Saturday and we know from his neighbour that Dan Hunter came fishing on Sunday. I'd be surprised if he was night fishing on a Sunday, so he should have gone home that evening ready for work the next morning. Any longer than that and I'd expect to see his body floating on the surface anyway.'

'How do you work that out?' asked Jane.

'It's all about gas. The water is still warm, so it'll slow the decaying process but not stop it. It should take three or four days for putrefaction to produce enough gas to make a body float this time of year.'

Jane looked surprised.

'We had a body in the Thames at Putney when I was in London.'

The scenes of crime officers, under Watson's guidance, began setting up arc lamps and a large tent around the fishing umbrella. Dixon could see the flashes of cameras all around. There was a need to work relatively quickly because rain was forecast. Jane Winter went back with Mr Wilkins to the farmhouse to take a statement from him while Dixon remained at the scene.

The divers arrived on schedule. There was still some light and a search of the immediate vicinity would be possible. At Dixon's request, PC Stevens had checked with the Environment Agency who had confirmed that the pumping station had been in operation on Monday and Tuesday morning. It was possible, therefore, that the body could have moved some way along the South Drain in the current. A more thorough search would be possible in the morning.

Within a few seconds of entering the water the divers reappeared giving the thumbs up signal. Dixon turned to PC Stevens.

'Better get the pathologist out here pronto.'

Dan Hunter's body was laid out on a tarpaulin on a level section of bank behind where he had been fishing. The scenes of crime officers immediately set up another tent covering his body.

'The pathologist will be here in half an hour, Sir,' said Stevens.

'Thank you, Constable.'

Dixon knelt over Dan Hunter's body. He guessed that Hunter had been lying face down in the water. His head was a livid black and blue and yet his hands were still the normal skin tone. There was otherwise very little evidence of putrefaction. The water had done its job. Dixon estimated that Hunter had been in the water for no more than two days, which gave a time of death of the previous Sunday afternoon, but the pathologist would no doubt be more precise.

There were no obvious signs of a struggle apart from a small bullet hole, or at least what looked like a small bullet hole, in the corner of Hunter's right eye. Dixon thought that it was possibly a .22 calibre pistol. He suspected that there would be an exit wound in the back of Hunter's head but he would need to wait for the pathologist to arrive to move the body further. This would certainly explain the blood spatter on the inside of the umbrella. He wondered whether a .22 calibre bullet would have killed Hunter on its own, but no doubt the pathologist would be able to confirm that too. At the very least, it would have incapacitated Hunter and he then either fell or was pushed into the South Drain. It was academic, of course, but Dixon guessed that Hunter had still been alive when he entered the water.

Jane Winter reappeared behind Dixon.

'Hunter?'

'Yes. Looks like a small bullet hole in his right eye. See it?'

'It's tiny.'

'Probably a .22 at close range.'

'Is there an exit wound?'

'I'll leave it to the pathologist to examine him. Must be, though. How else do you explain the blood on his brolly?'

'One thing's for sure.'

'What?'

'If there was any doubt about Jake's death, this one's definitely murder.'

'Is there any doubt about Jake's death?'

'Well, it's not as clear cut, is it?'

'No, I suppose not.'

'It tells me you're right about the drugs, though. Hunter wasn't involved in Jake's drug dealing, was he, so why kill him? It must be related to the birds' eggs.'

'Talking of birds, Jane, look at that.'

Dixon stood up and pointed across the fields on the far side of the Drain. A huge cloud of starlings was swirling in the dusk sky, illuminated only by the sun that was by now below the horizon. Tens of thousands of birds swooping and diving in concert, creating waves and shapes silhouetted against the red sky. They watched in silence for several minutes until the cloud dived towards the ground and disappeared.

'I'd heard about that but never seen it,' said Jane. 'The Somerset Levels are well known for it, apparently.'

'Certainly helps to pass the time while we wait for the pathologist,' replied Dixon.

'We're no nearer finding him though, are we, Sir?'

'Or her.'

Jane rolled her eyes.

'No, you're right, we're not,' said Dixon. 'We need to focus on what we know, I think.'

'Like what?'

'Well, Jake and Hunter were stealing peregrine falcon eggs, selling them in Dubai and making a lot of money doing it. Someone was setting up the deals and it would be reasonable to assume that they were taking a cut for doing so.'

'How d'you know someone else was involved?'

'I don't have any evidence, granted, but it must be right. Neither Jake nor Hunter could have done it themselves.'

'Not even over the Internet?'

'I doubt it. Let's hope High Tech find something on Jake's computer one way or the other. And then there's the person Jake was arguing with outside the Vic the night before he died. Who was that?'

'It's a shame Sarah Heath didn't get a good look at him.'

'It is.'

'We'll get a look at Hunter's computer now too, don't forget, Sir.'

PC Stevens appeared in the arc lights.

'Pathologist has arrived, Sir. PC Clarke is going to bring him out here.'

Dr Roger Poland was the senior forensic pathologist based at Musgrove Park Hospital, Taunton. He was a large man with greying hair and a direct manner evident from rather perfunctory introductions. Dixon decided that he liked him anyway and watched with Jane while he examined Hunter.

'Any idea how long?'

'He was last seen alive on Saturday afternoon as far as we know and there was no one fishing here on Saturday either, according to the farmer,' replied Dixon.

'Probably came fishing on Sunday, then?'

'It looks like it. He didn't turn up for work on Monday.'

'There's a small bullet hole in his right eye, probably a .22 calibre.' Poland rolled Hunter towards him and looked at the back of his head. 'And a corresponding exit wound just below and behind his left ear.'

'Is a .22 pistol powerful enough for that?' asked Dixon.

'There are a couple that could do it at close range, particularly if the bullet enters the skull through the eye socket. A Sig Sauer, perhaps.'

'Was it at close range?'

'Almost certainly. Judging by the angle, I'd say the victim was seated and the killer standing.'

'What about the bullet?'

'If he was sitting on that chair with the killer to his right then, on the angle, the bullet is almost certainly in the water.'

'One for the divers in the morning, then.'

'Good luck to them.'

'Would it have killed him instantly?'

'Does it matter?'

'I'm not sure that it does when you put it like that.'

'Possibly. I'll soon be able to tell if he was still alive when he went in when I open him up. I'll do the PM in the morning and let you have my report by lunchtime. OK?'

'Yes, thank you, Dr Poland.'

'You're the new chap?'

'Yes,' replied Dixon.

'We must have a beer sometime. And it's Roger, by the way.'

Chapter Ten

Dixon was late arriving at Bridgwater Police Station the following morning, having stopped off to break the news of Dan Hunter's murder to John and Maureen Fayter. DCI Lewis was waiting for him.

'Where have you been?'

'To see Jake's parents, Sir.'

'Fair enough,' replied Lewis. 'You let the girlfriend and her mother go?'

'I did. They've got nothing to do with it.'

'That's not what Steve Gorman thinks.'

'I was under the impression that I was in charge of this investigation, Sir.'

'You are.'

DCI Lewis waited for a response. Dixon had nothing further to add.

'So, what happens now?' asked Lewis.

'We follow up the leads that we have. We need to revisit the statements from the tourists in the gorge, chase up Hunter's bank statements. And I'm still waiting for High Tech's report on Jake's laptop and phone.'

'Anything interesting at Hunter's place?'

'Just an iPad, which is already with High Tech.'

'What about the man Fayter was arguing with the night before he died?'

'We're no nearer finding him at the moment. We'll be checking the CCTV and taking statements from the regulars at the Vic. There are two banks near there with cashpoints so it may be that they have some CCTV footage too.'

'Good. Get onto it straight away and let me know if you need any help. This is a double murder investigation now.'

'Yes, Sir.'

By mid-morning Dixon was sitting at his desk reading the report on Jake's laptop and iPhone that had finally arrived from the High Tech Unit. Steve Gorman and Mark Pearce were on their way to Birmingham to interview the tourists again and Jane Winter was chasing the banks for Dan Hunter's statements. She was also pursuing the CCTV footage from Burnham-on-Sea covering the evening before Jake's death.

The report gave a detailed forensic analysis of both the laptop and the iPhone and made a surprisingly interesting read. The laptop was a Sony Vaio, an old model that was still running Windows XP and IE8. The Internet history showed little of interest, except for several visits to a website offering advice on building a homemade incubator. Login details had been extracted for Facebook and Twitter accounts, giving both username and password. Dixon was aware of them from Jake's blog and was a Facebook friend and Twitter follower of both. Dixon thought it odd that there were no login details for Jake's blog and made a mental note to follow that up.

Jake's email was web based using an iMessage account. All of
the contacts had been extracted and accounted for. The Google
Chat facility had not been used. There was no Skype account or
similar. There were several folders of photographs, all of them
showing various climbing trips and routes, but no documents other
than the odd letter, which had been reproduced in the appendices
to the report.

The laptop had clearly been used for little more than photograph storage and occasional web surfing. It had revealed nothing
of real interest.

Dixon moved on to the section dealing with the iPhone. All of
the phone numbers for calls made and received had been extracted
and accounted for. There were numerous calls to and from Sarah and
Dan and also Jake's parents. There were also several calls to a number known to belong to Conrad Benton. Dixon noted something
else to be followed up later.

The iPhone email was set up with the same iMessage account.
There was no evidence that iMessages had ever been used and the
FaceTime contacts were only Sarah and Dan. The Facebook and
Twitter login details extracted from the Safari web browser on the
iPhone were the same as on the laptop.

High Tech had noted a word game similar to Scrabble called
Words With Friends, which included a chat facility but there was
no evidence that this had been used. In any event, the contacts list
included only Sarah and Dan. Apart from that, there were three
folders of photographs.

Jake's Facebook and Twitter accounts had been accessed and,
again, nothing of interest was found. In each case, no Facebook or
Twitter direct messages had been sent and Facebook chat had not
been used. The posts to Jake's Facebook timeline revealed nothing
of interest and Dixon had already seen his tweets.

Both the laptop and the iPhone had been the subject of detailed forensic analysis and had revealed nothing. Dixon vented his frustration on his biro and threw the broken pieces in the rubbish bin. Jake must have been communicating with the egg dealer, but they had not yet found the means by which he did so. Dixon was convinced this was the key. He opened his office door and shouted to Jane on the other side of the open plan office.

'Jane.'

'Yes, Sir.'

'Ring High Tech and tell 'em we must have their report on Dan Hunter's iPad by the end of today. Remind them this is a double murder investigation.'

'Yes, Sir.'

Dixon sat back down at his desk and picked up the report from High Tech again. He read it from start to finish for the second time. He was working on the basis that he might have missed something. The best part of an hour later he realised he had not. He reached over, picked up Jake's iPhone and ripped open the evidence bag. He placed it on the desk in front of him and then placed his own iPhone next to it. His own phone was switched on. He pressed the 'Home' button, entered the passcode and unlocked the Home screen. He sat staring at it for several minutes before picking up Jake's iPhone and switching it on. Unlike his own, Jake's was not password protected.

Jake's Home screen looked much like his own but there were subtle differences. There were all the standard icons for phone, music, mail, Internet and the like. There was also Newsstand. Dixon had never understood what Newsstand was for, nor had he ever worked out how to delete it. Jake had also installed the Climber Magazine app and the Crags Climbing Log Book. Dixon looked up the police station Wi-Fi password and connected Jake's iPhone to the Internet. He then returned to the Home screen.

Jake had not received any email but the 'App Store' icon was displaying an update alert. The figure 1 in a red circle at the top right corner of the icon indicated that one app needed updating. Dixon touched the 'App Store' icon and opened the Updates screen. It showed a Twitter app requiring an update and gave the new version number. Dixon pressed the 'Home' button and returned to the Home screen. He then tapped the Photos icon and spent five minutes looking at Jake's photos. All of them climbing photographs. He recognised the sea cliffs at Gogarth, the Dinorwic slate quarries and, inevitably, Cheddar Gorge.

His mind wandered back to climbing on the slate. It had always suited him. The rock was rarely vertical and it was possible to stay in balance on the tiniest of foot and handholds. Jake had enjoyed climbing on slate, too, and had proved to be exceptionally good at it, bagging a number of outstanding second ascents. Dixon remembered a whole week spent ticking all of the routes on the Rainbow Slab, including a second ascent by Jake of Raped by Affection (E7 6c).

There was a knock at Dixon's office door.

'Come in, Jane.'

'We've got Hunter's bank statements, Sir.'

'Well?'

'He has two accounts with Barclays in Burnham. A current account with small change in it and a savings account with just under one hundred and forty grand.'

'That's a lot of money for a divorced postman, wouldn't you say? Do we know when it arrived?'

'17th May. The bank checked with him and he told them it was an inheritance, apparently.'

'I bet he did. That's the money from the second trip to Dubai.'

'Looks like it.'

'Well, now we know why Dan was killed. And it's reasonable to assume we're sitting on what the killer wants.'

'We are.'

'Get back onto the bank and find out where that money came from, will you?'

'They're coming back to me with that information. Anything on the laptop or phone?'

'Not really, no. You have a read of it, see what you think.' Dixon handed her the report.

'Yes, Sir.'

'I'd better take Monty for a walk.'

———

Dixon arrived back from Victoria Park to find Dan Hunter's post mortem report on his desk. Single gunshot wound to the head. Dan had been alive when he entered the water but, almost certainly, unconscious. The time of death was given as between 1 p.m. and 4 p.m. on Sunday afternoon. Nothing new.

Dixon spent the rest of the afternoon watching the CCTV footage from Burnham the evening before Jake's death. There was extensive coverage, which the local CCTV Control Team had provided. It included Automatic Number Plate Recognition but, sadly, this did not make it any more interesting. There was over nine hours of footage in total from four different cameras. Not only that, but Barclays and NatWest had also been able to recover the footage from their cashpoint cameras and a police constable had been despatched to collect it.

Dixon watched with his finger hovering over the 'Fast Forward' button. After nearly three hours he had seen nothing of note. He stopped the tape, went back to his office and sent an email to DCI Lewis asking for a junior officer to assist with reviewing the CCTV footage. He then shouted across to Jane.

'Fancy a drink, Jane?'

'Yes, Sir. Where are we going?'

'The Vic.'

Dixon drove out through Bridgwater and headed north on the A38.

'We'll stay off the motorway, I think. What did you make of the High Tech report?'

'Disappointing. I was hoping there'd be some email or chat exchange with our man.'

'Me too.'

'Maybe all of the contact was in person?' asked Jane.

'If it was we're in deep trouble. The only person who could identify the dealer was Hunter.'

'That would explain why he was killed?'

'It would. But then so would the money.'

'True.'

'We'll see what we find in the Vic, but I'm not holding my breath. The CCTV is the better bet but we're not entirely sure what we're looking for, are we?'

'No, Sir.'

Dixon was deep in thought. Suddenly, he thumped the steering wheel with the palm of his hand.

'Oh, shit.'

He stamped on the brakes and swerved into the entrance to the British Car Auctions depot. The car behind swerved to avoid him and hooted its horn in a loud blast. Dixon spun the Land Rover around and was trying to cross the northbound traffic and head south.

'What is it?' asked Jane.

'Was there any mention of a Twitter app in the High Tech report on Jake's iPhone?'

'No, there was a Twitter account but no app. There were some climbing apps and Words With Friends but he hadn't installed the Twitter app.'

'Yes, he had,' said Dixon, spinning his wheels as he sped across the line of northbound traffic and headed south. 'I looked at his phone. There was an App Store Update alert and it was Twitter.'

'But it may be for the same account?' said Jane.

'We'll soon see.'

They were back at Bridgwater Police Station within ten minutes. Dixon retrieved Jake's iPhone from the evidence store and switched it on while he walked up to his office. Jane was waiting for him in his office.

'Are you familiar with this Twitter app?'

'No, Sir, sorry.'

Dixon unlocked Jake's iPhone and looked at the Home screen. There was no Twitter app icon. He showed it to Jane.

'Try the utilities folder,' she said.

Dixon touched the utilities folder icon and there it was, the familiar blue square with a white songbird in flight. Without hesitation, Dixon opened the app.

'Will it work if it's not connected to the Internet?' asked Jane.

'It's opened but I don't think it will update, that's all.'

Dixon placed the iPhone on his desk and sat in his chair. Jane was standing behind him looking over his shoulder.

The app opened at the home page, which displayed tweets from users Jake had been following. It had not been opened for some time, as evidenced by the most recent tweet being timed seventeen days ago. Dixon had never really understood Twitter and skipped the @Connect and #Discover icons, opening instead the section called 'Me'. This displayed Jake's full name and username, the number of tweets, following and followers, as well as the 'Account Settings' button. There was a direct messages icon in the form of a grey envelope on a white background. Next to Settings was an icon Dixon did not recognise. It looked like the head and shoulders of two people in silhouette. Dixon pointed to it.

'What's that one?'

'No idea, Sir. Open it and see.'

Dixon tapped the icon. The screen turned clockwise to reveal a new page headed 'Accounts'. There were two. Dixon recognised the first. It was the account detailed in the High Tech Unit report. The second account was new. The full name was Armitage Shanks and the username @NewSlatesman. Dixon tapped the screen and it rotated anticlockwise to reveal the new Twitter account.

'You crafty bugger, Jake,' muttered Dixon.

'He had a second Twitter account?'

'He did. And someone in High Tech needs their arse kicking. New Slatesman is a rock climb in the slate quarries in North Wales. Jake got the second ascent last year.'

'What about Armitage Shanks?'

'We were in town, years ago, and got stopped by someone with a petition. Jake gave his name then as Armitage Shanks. They make loos.'

'I know that, Sir.'

'Funny thing is, when it was my turn to the sign the petition, I gave my name as Jake Fayter. He never forgave me for that.' Dixon smiled.

He tapped the 'Me' icon.

'He's only following two people and got two followers, look,' said Jane.

'And they're the same people. A private party, perhaps?'

The first account belonged to Desperate Dan with the username @Quarryman1971.

'I'm assuming Dan Hunter was born in 1971?'

'He was, Sir. What's the significance of Quarryman?'

'Another climb on the slate. Take a look at the second account. Get it?'

'Perry Falco and @DuckHawkMan. Doesn't mean anything to me,' said Jane.

'*Falco peregrinus* is the Latin name for the peregrine falcon and duck hawk is the American name for it. That, Jane, is our dealer.'

'Can we get Twitter to tell us who he is then?'

'I doubt it. Fake name. Probably a fake email too and I bet he's hidden his IP address behind any number of proxy servers.'

'Could be abroad even?'

'Well, he wasn't when he stood next to Dan Hunter and shot him in the eye.'

'True.'

Dixon looked at all three accounts. None had ever tweeted.

'Must be direct messages then,' he said. He returned to the 'Me' screen and tapped the grey envelope. This revealed a page entitled Messages. There was only one entry, an exchange started by Perry Falco @DuckHawkMan. It was not recent, as evidenced by the '198d' adjacent to it.

'One hundred and ninety-eight days ago, I suppose?' asked Jane.

'Beginning of April at a guess,' said Dixon. He tapped the arrow to open the message string. 'This is it.' Dixon reached for a pen and paper and wrote out the messages exactly as they appeared on the screen.

09/04 09:34

*Millennium girls
birthday 27 November*

09/04 19:17

*Wish them a Happy Birthday
from me*

10/04 10.02

Ring me on 313050

10/04 17:12

*Will do. Give me a couple
of days*

13/04 20:46

Well?

14/04 07:32

We are in luck

14/04 15:49

*Party starts Manchester on 17th.
Entry code EK018.
You'll be met*

18/04 21:20

Great party. Loving it!

30/04 09:12

Fancy another trip?

30/04 14:43

Yes!

02/05 08:14

Same birthday. Ring me on
312100

05/05 20:12

On way to Manchester.
Same entry code?

05/05 21:42

Yes. All booked

'It's a load of crap.'

'Code is the word you're looking for, Jane. It's a load of code.'

'What for?'

'That's what we need to find out, isn't it? For starters, I'll bet you a tenner that Manchester EK018 is a flight number. What price Manchester to Dubai?'

Dixon opened Google on his computer and typed in EK018.

'There we are. Manchester to Dubai daily. Emirates flight 18. An A380 no less.'

'So, they flew from Manchester to Dubai on 17th April.'

'Better check with Emirates. And find out who booked and paid for those flights.'

'Now?'

Dixon looked at his watch. It was nearly 7 p.m.

'No, in the morning will do. You head off home.'

'Yes, Sir. What about the rest of it?'

'Setting up the two egg stealing trips, I expect.'

'Not the most elaborate code, is it?'

'Probably never expected anyone to read it. They just dressed the messages up as innocuous crap that wouldn't attract attention. Easily lost in the billions of direct messages passing daily on Twitter.'

Jane went home leaving Dixon sitting at his desk. He turned back to the piece of paper in front of him. He had always hated crosswords, particularly cryptic ones. The millennium girls' birthday on 27th November was clearly significant, whoever the millennium girls were, as were the telephone numbers with no dialling code. Most importantly, though, he now had proof of the dealer's existence.

Dixon looked at Jake's iPhone. It was his only means of communication with @DuckHawkMan, unless he could follow him on Twitter. He turned back to his computer and went to twitter.com /duckhawkman.

@DuckHawkMan's tweets are protected.
Only confirmed followers have access to @duckhawkman's Tweets and complete profile. Click the "Follow" button to send a follow request.

'Fuck it.'

Dixon did not hold out much hope of a follow request being accepted and, without the password, his only access to the second Twitter account was through the app on Jake's iPhone. He made up his mind quickly. He put the empty evidence bag in the bottom drawer of his desk, slipped Jake's phone into his jacket pocket and went home.

———⌣———

Dixon drove north on the A38. He was not entirely comfortable with his decision to take Jake's iPhone but consoled himself with the knowledge that he needed to move quickly. Various clichés occurred to him, that the end would justify the means and an unfortunate one involving omelettes and breaking eggs. But there was no escaping the simple fact that he had crossed the line. At worst, it would involve a disciplinary process and a reprimand. At best, he would get away with it. It was a risk worth taking.

He stopped off at the Chinese takeaway in Burnham-on-Sea and managed to fit in ten minutes on the beach with Monty while his food was being cooked. There was a full moon, which made Monty visible in the dark. It was one advantage of a white dog.

Dixon was home by 8.30 p.m. He fed Monty and then set about his takeaway. In between mouthfuls of chow mein, he opened a can of lager, powered up his laptop and switched on the TV. He opted for *The Wild Geese*. It was a film he had seen many times and it helped him think.

He opened Internet Explorer and typed '313050' into Google. The results were disappointing. He scrolled down through entries that meant very little to him, a hex colour code, whatever that was, and what appeared to be a zip code in Denver. The last entry on the first page was more promising and came from streetmap.co.uk. Dixon clicked on it and found himself looking at a map of Shrewsbury. He scrolled down looking for further information and clicked on a link to 'convert coordinates'. This opened a new window, which gave easting, northing, postcode, latitude and longitude, and grid reference. Dixon did not recognise the other entries.

Dixon could see that 313050 was the northing. He recognised the grid reference format, SJ 500 103, but was unfamiliar with northing and easting. He went back to Google and typed in 'northing'. Within a few clicks he was on Wikipedia learning about all-numeric grid references, 'quoted as pairs of numbers'.

'Pairs of numbers' was the key. He looked again at the first of the Twitter direct messages, 'millennium girls birthday 27 November'. He wrote down 271100 next to it on the piece of paper. It had to be the first part of an all-numeric grid reference.

He was on gridreferencefinder.com in a matter of seconds. He entered 271100 for the easting and 313050 for the northing and clicked 'Go'. Moments later he was looking at an aerial view of Cader Idris in the Snowdonia National Park. Next he entered 271100 and 312100 and found himself at the foot of the Pencoed Pillar, again, in the Cader Idris region of Snowdonia.

Dixon reached for Jake's iPhone. He opened the Twitter app, navigated to direct messages and tapped out a message to @DuckHawkMan.

I've got your money.

He took a large swig of lager and clicked 'Send'. It was going to be a long night.

The reply came within minutes.

Who is this?

Dixon was stunned. He had not expected a response at all, let alone one so quickly. He was suddenly aware of the implications of what he had done and what he was doing. He had removed evidence in a double murder investigation and, if he was right, was now in direct contact with the man who had put a gun to Dan Hunter's head and pulled the trigger. He was also the man who had killed Jake.

He took a swig of lager and turned his attention to his response. An honest answer to the question was not an option. 'This is Detective Inspector Nick Dixon, Avon and Somerset CID' would bring the exchange to an abrupt halt. Any chance of finding DuckHawkMan would be gone in an instant. The obvious answer was to masquerade as Sarah Heath. It would be entirely plausible that Jake's girlfriend would have access to his Twitter accounts. It would be equally plausible that she had access to the money from the second Dubai trip. This might be the means of bringing DuckHawkMan out into the open.

Dixon reached for Jake's iPhone, which was on the arm of the sofa. His hand was shaking. He suddenly became aware that his heart was beating loud and fast. He took a deep breath and began tapping out a reply.

Sarah Heath.

His finger hovered over the 'Send' button. He hesitated. It occurred to him that DuckHawkMan might know where Sarah lived. If he knew Jake, it would be reasonable to assume that he knew where Jake lived and that would lead him to Sarah. He might even know where she worked. The answer was obvious. Dixon needed Sarah's cooperation. He threw what was left of his chow mein in the bin, picked up his car keys and set off towards Burnham.

He had no real idea how he was going to persuade Sarah to cooperate, particularly after the hard time he had given her in interview. Not only that, but as far as she was concerned, Jake had killed her sister. It was certainly not going to be easy, but he had to try. Not least for Dan Hunter's sake.

Dixon parked in the car park in front of the Clarence and went into the public bar. No sign of Sarah. He found her behind the lounge bar. It was empty apart from an elderly couple in the far corner. Sarah was changing the gin optic and had her back to him when he walked in.

'I'll have a pint of lager, please, Sarah,' said Dixon. 'Can I get you anything?'

Sarah's smile disappeared immediately she recognised Dixon.

'What do you want?'

'I need your help . . .'

'My help? You need my help?'

'Yes. Let me buy you a drink and I can explain.'

'You've got a bloody cheek after the grilling you gave me. You practically accused me of killing Jake.'

'I've never thought you had anything to do with his death. You know that.'

'What was all that about then?'

'It's a murder investigation. You were withholding information. What was I supposed to do?'

Sarah banged Dixon's pint down on the bar.

'Ten minutes, that's all I need.'

'Why should I?'

'For Jake.'

'He killed my sister.'

'Did he? Are you sure about that? Because I'm not. All we've got is one statement from a known drug dealer with a list of previous convictions as long as your arm. Hardly compelling evidence, is it?'

Sarah ignored him.

Dixon continued. 'No jury would convict on that evidence. And let's be honest, Sarah, if Jenna hadn't bought the drugs off Jake, she'd have got them off someone else, wouldn't she?'

Sarah began pouring herself a glass of white wine.

'That's £6.10 including the wine.'

Dixon took his wallet out of his back pocket and produced a ten pound note. Sarah gave him his change, picked up her glass of wine and walked around into the seating area. She sat down at the table adjacent to the bar. Dixon sat on the bar stool opposite her.

'Go on. I'm listening.'

Dixon placed Jake's iPhone on the table in front of Sarah.

'Whose is that?'

'It's Jake's. I asked you about the dealer, the man setting up the egg deals in Dubai. Remember?'

'Yes.'

'You said you didn't know him or how Jake was contacting him?'

'That's right.'

'Jake was using a second Twitter account hidden behind his main account in the Twitter app installed on this phone. They were using Twitter direct messaging. Look.'

Dixon showed her the Twitter account and the string of direct messages.

'Those messages don't make any sense.'

'It's a basic code of sorts. There are all-numeric grid references and flight numbers in there.'

'So, what can I do?'

'I need you out of the way for a few days.'

'Out of the way?'

'Yes. That's it. That's all you have to do. Disappear.'

'Why?'

'I think this dealer, this DuckHawkMan, is the one who untied Jake's ropes and shot Dan.'

'Dan's dead?'

'I'm afraid he is. He was shot in the head at point blank range and pushed into the South Drain on Sunday afternoon.'

'Shit . . .'

'I need to convince this man that I've got the money, Sarah. That's what this is all about, the money. To do that, I need to pretend to be you.'

'Me?'

'Who else would have access to the money? I need to pretend to be you so I can bring this fucker out into the open.'

'But why do I have to disappear?'

'What if he knows where you live? We know he's got a gun and he's prepared to use it.'

'You're kidding me?'

'No, I'm not. Look, I pretend to be you, arrange a meeting with him, he turns up and we've got him. But I need to know you're safely out of the way.'

Sarah shook her head.

'I cannot take any risks with your safety. He may come after you anyway if he thinks you've got the money.'

'But there's nowhere I can go.'

'You can stay at my cottage in Brent Knoll.'

'Do I have a choice?'

'You do. You could say no but then, at best, a double murderer walks away.'

'And at worst?'

'He comes looking for you.'

'You're fucking kidding me.'

Sarah started to cry.

'I don't have a lot of choice, do I?'

'Good. You'll be fine.'

'What about work?'

'Leave them to me. Has this place got Wi-Fi?'

'Yes. It's free.'

Dixon connected Jake's iPhone to the Internet, navigated to Twitter direct messaging and retyped the direct message.

Sarah.

His finger hovered over the 'Send' button.

'Are you sure?'

'Yes.'

———

It took Dixon no more than five minutes to explain to the owner of the Clarence that he was taking Sarah Heath into protective custody. They left quickly and drove north along the seafront, turned left along Berrow Road and then right into Rectory Road.

'Where are we going?'

'We'll take the back roads. Safer.'

'But I need some stuff from my flat. Clothes and . . .'

'Too risky. He could be watching it by now. I've got some clothes you can borrow and I'm sure police expenses will stretch to a new toothbrush.'

Sarah shrugged.

'Have you eaten?'

'Yes.'

'Good. I've already been in the Chinese once today.'

They drove the rest of the way in silence.

Dixon rented a small end terraced cottage opposite and one hundred yards along Brent Street from the Red Cow in Brent

Knoll. The front door at the side of the cottage and the parking at the back were accessed via an alleyway between the cottages. Dixon drove round behind the cottage, parked and switched off the engine.

'I hope you're a dog person.'

'Not really.'

'You'll be fine. He's soft as a mop.'

'Who is?'

'Monty.'

Monty took an instant shine to Sarah and, once the introductions were over, Dixon showed Sarah to the bedroom upstairs and gave her some clean sheets for the bed.

'He's lovely,' she said.

'He is. I wouldn't want to be a burglar, though.'

'I feel better already.'

'I'll be on the sofa. Keep the bedroom door shut or you'll be sharing the bed with him.'

'I will.'

Dixon sat on the sofa and connected Jake's iPhone to the Internet. He checked the Twitter direct messages. There was a reply waiting for him.

What do you want?

Sarah appeared at the top of the stairs. She could see Dixon looking at Jake's iPhone.

'Got a reply?'

'Yes. He wants to know what you want.'

'What do I want, then?' asked Sarah.

'I reckon you'd want Jake's share of the money?'

'And to be left alone.'

'Good thinking.'

Dixon looked back to the iPhone and began typing a reply.

Jake's share.

Dixon tapped 'Send'. He waited a few seconds and then began typing another message.

and to be left alone

He sent the second message, put the iPhone on the arm of the sofa and looked across to Sarah, who was now at the bottom of the stairs.

'Tea?'

'Nothing stronger?'

'Lager?'

'That'll have to do.'

Dixon went into the kitchen to fetch a lager from the fridge. Sarah looked at a pile of DVDs on a cardboard box next to the TV.

'I hope to God there's something decent on the telly. Your DVD collection stinks.'

'Thanks for that.'

Dixon handed a can of lager and a glass to Sarah. Then he picked up Jake's iPhone and checked for a reply.

Agreed. I'll come to
the Clarence tomorrow.

'Oh, bugger.'

'What's the problem?'

'He wants to meet you at the Clarence tomorrow.'

'That's just fucking great, that is. He's got a gun, for fuck's sake.'

'He's not going to meet you, is he? You'll be safely tucked up here. Just leave it to me.'

'Dennis is going to love this.'

'Dennis is the owner, isn't he?'

'Yes.'

'What time does the bar open?'

'11 a.m. The lounge bar is always open for residents, though.'

'Are there any at the moment?'

'Two couples, I think.'

'CCTV?'

'In the public bar. There isn't any in the lounge bar.'

Dixon tapped out a reply.

*Come at 10.30 a.m. Use the back
door. I'll be in the public bar.*

'We can keep the residents upstairs and the bar will be empty. Perfect.'

'What about the gun?'

'We'll let the armed response boys worry about that.'

That was a white lie. Dixon had already decided there would be no backup. He'd have to keep him talking until the armed response team arrived. It was a risk worth taking, he thought. And he reminded himself that it was only a .22 calibre pistol. That would not be much consolation to Dan Hunter, but it was the best Dixon was going to get.

Chapter Eleven

Dixon woke early after an uncomfortable night on the sofa. He was grateful that he had kept his old sleeping bag, otherwise it would have been cold as well. It was still dark. He reached for his phone and rang Jane Winter.

'Jane, it's Nick. Where are you?'

'In bed.'

'Get out sharpish, will you? I need you to get over to my place as quickly as you can. Swing by the station on the way and pick up two sets of body armour.'

'Body armour?'

'I'll explain when you get here. And tell no one.'

'What's going on?'

'Ring me when you get to the Red Cow. Do you know it?'

'Yes.'

Jane was about to ask another question when Dixon rang off.

Jane arrived at Dixon's cottage just before 8 a.m. She parked in the road fifty yards down from the cottage and walked back. Monty alerted Dixon and Sarah Heath to her arrival before Jane knocked on the door.

'Where's the body armour?'

'In my car.'

'Well done.'

Jane spotted Sarah in the kitchen and raised her eyebrows.

'Protective custody,' said Dixon. 'Monty and I spent a very uncomfortable night on the sofa. Coffee?'

'Coffee and an explanation, please.'

'This is Jake's.'

Dixon handed Jake's iPhone to Jane and left her reading the exchange of Twitter direct messages with @DuckHawkMan while he made the coffee.

Jane shouted through to the kitchen. 'You are in deep shit.'

'Possibly.'

Dixon appeared with two mugs of coffee.

'This is evidence,' said Jane, jabbing her finger at Jake's iPhone.

'It is.'

'And you've set up a meeting with a murderer. An armed murderer.'

'I have.'

'He's coming to a public house at 10.30 today expecting to meet Sarah,' said Jane, nodding in the direction of Sarah Heath, who was maintaining a discreet silence in the kitchen. 'And he's expecting to collect seventy grand.'

'He is. And instead he's going to meet you and me.'

'Me?'

'Unless you'd rather not get involved. I'd understand.'

'We should call this in.'

'No.'

'No?'

'It's not an option. Look, there's no need for you to take the risk. You stay here. I'll see to it you're in the clear if the shit hits the fan.'

'In the clear?'

'Yes.'

'I'm not letting you go in there on your own. End of,' said Jane.

'Thank you.'

'But if this goes wrong, we are in deep trouble.'

'It won't.'

Jane forced a nervous smile.

'And if it does, they'll throw the book at me. You were following orders,' said Dixon.

Dixon and Jane left Sarah Heath at the cottage with Monty and arrived in Burnham-on-Sea just after 9 a.m. They parked in Herbert Road to keep Dixon's Land Rover out of sight and walked along the beach to the Royal Clarence Hotel.

Explaining the situation to Dennis, the owner, made for an uncomfortable meeting but he agreed to cooperate, albeit reluctantly. Two couples were staying at the hotel. Both had already finished breakfast and would be out for the day by 10 a.m. By 10.15 a.m. everyone else would be upstairs, leaving only Dixon and Jane on the ground floor. The front door would be locked, as usual, leaving only the back door open. The door at the bottom of the stairs would also be locked.

Jane would be positioned behind the public bar and Dixon would be waiting in the office between the back door and the bar. With the door shut, he would be hidden but CCTV would give him a clear view of the back door and rear courtyard as well as the bar area and front door. Both wore body armour, Jane under a baggy top and Dixon under his jacket.

'I still don't understand why we can't call it in.'

'Trust me, Jane. He's not going to kill a police officer.'

Jane was about to ask another question when Dixon looked at his watch and spoke.

'Ten minutes. Better get in position. Chop lemons or something, and remember to get down behind the bar if he produces the gun. OK?'

'Yes, Sir.'

'Good luck.'

Dixon waited in the office watching the CCTV of the rear courtyard and back door. He could see Jane at the bar. She had finished chopping lemons and was now arranging the mixers. Dixon checked his watch. 10.30 a.m. had come and gone and it was nearly 10.40 a.m. He rang Sarah Heath.

'Sarah, it's Nick. Everything all right?'

'Fine. No sign?'

'Not yet. Better go.'

Dixon rang off. He checked his watch: 10.45 a.m. His mind was racing.

Where the fuck is he?

Was he coming at all?

Was he late?

Was he waiting for the bar to open?

Had he smelled a rat?

Dixon could live with the consequences of a reprimand or worse but he needed a result to justify it, not least to himself. Consequences. Sarah Heath would need to remain in protective custody. He was not going to be popular. And then there was @DuckHawkMan.

Suddenly, a figure appeared at the front door. He tried the door. It was locked. Dixon checked his watch. 10.47 a.m. It could be a pisshead after an early drink. The bar was due to open at 11 a.m.

The same figure appeared in the courtyard at the back of the hotel a few seconds later. Tentative at first. He had a good look around and then made for the back door. Dixon reached for the phone and dialled 999.

'This is 3275 Detective Inspector Nick Dixon, Bridgwater CID. I need immediate assistance at the Royal Clarence Hotel, Burnham-on-Sea.' He spoke quietly and quickly. 'I have an armed man in the public bar. He has a gun. Send an armed response unit and an ambulance.' Dixon waited long enough for an acknowledgement from the operator before he rang off.

Dixon saw the figure appear on camera in the public bar. He opened the door of the office quietly and made for the door to the bar.

Jane had her back to the bar.

'I'm looking for Sarah Heath.'

Jane turned round.

'Steve, what are you doing here?'

Dixon appeared in the doorway.

'He's here for his money. Aren't you, Steve?'

Steve Gorman was wearing dark trousers, a polo shirt and a black leather jacket. He turned to face Dixon.

'I'm here to help. I heard about it on the radio.'

'It's not been on the radio.'

Gorman looked at Jane and then back to Dixon. He shook his head. He opened his mouth to speak but said nothing. Dixon broke the silence.

'"They're peregrine falcons, Sir. There's a pair nesting on Priest Rock." Remember, Steve?'

'Anyone can spot a peregrine falcon, for fuck's sake. That doesn't mean a thing.'

'Doesn't it?' said Dixon. 'Maybe not on its own but what with everything else . . .'

'What else?' demanded Gorman.

'Who was it who said "too many tweets make a twat"?'

Gorman was red in the face. He looked nervously from Dixon to Jane and back to Dixon. He stepped back into a table and chairs but kept his footing.

'You still haven't explained what you're doing here,' said Dixon.

Gorman did not respond.

Dixon moved to his right, pulled a chair out from under a table and sat down facing Gorman.

'You're investigating the death of Jenna Williams. But your main suspect is your partner in crime. You can't arrest him without risking everything. Let's assume he threatened to blab about the egg dealing. You argued outside the Vic, perhaps. That was you, wasn't it?'

No reply. Dixon continued.

'So you killed him.'

'I didn't kill Fayter.'

'You waited until his weight was off the ropes, untied them and watched him fall to his death.'

'I did not kill Jake Fayter.'

'You even told Tina Williams that Jake killed her daughter in the hope she'd kill him . . .'

'No, that was a mistake.'

'Convenient, then, wasn't it?'

'He spat in my face. "Arrest me and you're fucked," he said. But I didn't kill him. And yes, it was convenient. Fucking convenient. I couldn't believe my luck.'

'So what about Dan Hunter? Just about the money, was it?'

Gorman had begun to cry. Tears were streaming down his cheeks. He was salivating profusely. Air bubbles were appearing and disappearing on each breath.

'Good old fashioned greed, Steve.'

'The greedy little fucker.' Gorman was talking almost to himself. 'He was blackmailing me. What else could I do?'

The realisation of what he had said suddenly dawned on Steve Gorman. He reached into his inside jacket pocket and produced a gun. He pointed it first at Dixon then at Jane then back to Dixon.

'Will we need Ballistics to confirm that is the same gun that killed Dan Hunter?'

'No.'

Dixon pointed to the CCTV camera above and to the right of the bar.

'Smile for the camera.'

Gorman pointed the gun at the camera and fired. The camera disintegrated.

'That was unwise. There's an armed response unit upstairs and another behind the sea wall.'

Gorman was sobbing uncontrollably. 'Fuck, fuck, fuck.' He began to shake.

'Put the gun down, Steve. You're not going anywhere.'

A siren could be heard in the distance.

'You said they were upstairs.'

'I lied.'

Gorman pointed the gun at Jane. Dixon sat up in his chair. The siren was getting louder.

'They'll be here before you can reach the door, Steve. And where do you think you're going to go? Put the gun down.'

'I can't go to prison.'

'Think about it. You didn't kill Jake. That just leaves Dan Hunter. You'd get parole in fifteen to twenty years.'

'I can't go to prison.'

Suddenly, Gorman stopped shaking. When he spoke, he was quite calm.

'Tell my children I love them.'

Both Dixon and Jane would later testify that what happened next was in slow motion. Gorman turned first to Jane.

'Goodbye, Jane.'

Then he turned to Dixon.

'Goodbye, Sir.'

Then he placed the barrel of the pistol to his right temple and pulled the trigger. Dixon lunged forward from his chair but was too late to stop him. Jane turned away but was too late to avoid being spattered with blood and brain, which sprayed across the bar.

The gun fell to the ground. Gorman gave a faint smile and then dropped to his knees. His mouth opened as if he was about to speak and he exhaled. Then he fell forward.

Dixon could see Jane screaming but heard nothing. The first sound he was aware of was a battering ram at the front door of the hotel. Suddenly the bar was full of uniformed police officers. Dixon was not aware that he was speaking but could hear his own voice.

'I am DI Nick Dixon. That is DC Jane Winter. The gun is over there. This is DS Steve Gorman. He needs an ambulance.'

_____

Dixon and Jane sat outside with a drink and watched through a window at the front of the hotel while the paramedics worked on Gorman. They watched as the paramedics sat back, looked at each other and shook their heads. Detective Sergeant Steven Gorman was pronounced dead at the scene.

The seafront had been sealed off and the hotel evacuated. It was likely to be some time before the bar would open to the public again. A thorough clean would be required.

DCI Lewis arrived before Dixon had finished his drink.

'Steve Gorman?'

'I'm afraid so, Sir.'

'He killed Fayter and Hunter?'

'He admitted killing Hunter but was adamant he didn't kill Jake.'

'Did he kill him?'

'I thought so, Sir, but I'm not so sure now.'

'So, who did then?'

'I don't know.'

'But he was behind the egg dealing?'

'He was.'

'Fucking hell. We'll have to keep this quiet.'

'Well, there's not going to be a trial.'

'He's dead?'

'Yes, Sir.'

Lewis shook his head.

'Let me have your statements then take a couple of days off, the pair of you. I'll sort this mess out.'

<hr />

They collected Sarah Heath from Dixon's cottage and dropped her at her mother's house in East Huntspill on their way to Bridgwater. Dixon then spent twenty minutes waiting outside Jane's flat while she showered and changed clothes. They finally arrived at Bridgwater Police Station just before lunch.

They spent the rest of the day completing their witness statements. Dixon gave a detailed account of the use of Jake's iPhone in setting up the meeting with Gorman but Jane made no mention of it. Otherwise, their statements were almost identical. They handed the statements to DCI Lewis just before 5 p.m. and left the station together.

'What about Jake?' asked Jane.

'We'll worry about him next week, Jane. And Conrad bloody Benton.'

Jane nodded.

'You shouldn't be on your own. Is there anywhere you can go?'

'No.'

'Looks like it's Monty and me on the sofa again. C'mon, let's get a bottle of wine.'

Jane smiled. 'How about two?'

———⌣———

DCI Lewis rang before they reached Brent Knoll.

'I've read your statement, Nick.'

'Yes, Sir.'

'The end can sometimes justify the means. But we have procedures for a reason.'

'Yes, Sir.'

'We understand each other, I think, so we'll say no more about it this time.'

'Thank you, Sir.'

Dixon rang off, turned to Jane and smiled.

'We're off the hook . . .'

Chapter Twelve

Late on the Sunday afternoon Dixon was walking on Burnham Beach with Monty. They had parked at the end of Allandale Road and walked out to the lighthouse, which was silhouetted against the evening sky as they approached. The tide was out and seagulls were wandering up and down in the channels between the sand banks looking for worms. Monty was tearing up and down after his tennis ball, as usual.

Dixon had always loved the Burnham lighthouse. It was not a conventional lighthouse by any means. It was square, for a start, and stood in the middle of the beach on nine stilts. It had been a part of Dixon's life since he had first used it for goalposts as a child. He stood at the foot of one of the stilts, looking at the steel plates bolted to it, and remembered challenging Jake to climb up to the door using the bolts for finger holds. Neither of them had got close to it but it had been fun trying.

Dixon heard the familiar soft ping of an email arriving.

He walked up the beach towards the dunes intending to sit on one of the concrete blocks that had once been part of sea defences long since smashed to pieces. He took out his phone and checked his email while he walked.

jakefayter [New Post] I'm Sorry – jakefayter posted

The subject line was enough to stop Dixon in his tracks. He recognised the familiar email alert for a new post on Jake's blog. It would be interesting to know when Jake had written it but that could wait. Dixon sat on a concrete block and opened the email. He knew instinctively what was coming. He felt tears falling slowly down his cheeks.

I'm Sorry.

If you are reading this then I am already dead. A horrible cliché that, I know, but it's true. I've rescheduled this post twice already so if it's live, I'm not.

I've done something that I cannot live with. I have tried. God knows, I've tried. But I just cannot see a way through what I have done. All I can say is sorry to everyone I have let down and everyone I have hurt.

I have been making a few quid selling ecstasy. This one time I was sold PMA. I didn't know what it was. If I had done, things might have been different. Anyway, I sold it to Jenna and she died.

Sarah, please believe me that I am sorry. I had no idea what PMA was and I would never have sold it to Jenna had I known. Please believe me and please tell Tina that I am sorry.

I have let everyone down, including my parents. I love you both and am truly sorry for not being a better son.

Nick and I used to talk about soloing the north face of the Eiger in flip-flops when our time came. Better to die in a climbing accident than suicide. So, here's what I am going to do. I'm going to tie my ropes in a loose granny knot and take my chances abseiling over High Rock. When my time comes I won't know much about it and at least I won't directly have taken my own life.

Maybe that's my final act of cowardice. Who knows? I only ask your forgiveness, please, on all counts.

I love you all.

Jake

PS Tell Nick I changed my mind about 'Never Mind the Bollocks'. They were the best of days, matey. I'll see you on the other side. J.

Acknowledgements

First of all, a big thank you for reading this book. It's a terrifying experience to publish your first novel and then truly humbling to find that people are actually reading it and liking it. A real roller coaster.

I'd been carrying *As the Crow Flies* around in my head for a good few years before finally summoning up the courage to make a start in October 2012. Much of the climbing is semi-autobiographical, with perhaps a touch of exaggeration thrown in. I prefer to call it 'poetic licence'! They really were happy days.

What about Burnham-on-Sea? It's a seaside town in Somerset and my home for the first 32 years of my life. It's a great place, with great people and some atmospheric scenery for setting a bit of crime fiction. I love it. If you're ever passing by on the M5, drop in and have a bag of chips on the seafront.

I live in Devon with my wife and two dogs now but still regard Burnham-on-Sea as home. You can regularly find me on the beach with my dogs or wandering about with my Dictaphone in hand, doing a bit of research for my next book.

Finally, if you enjoyed *As the Crow Flies*, I'd be very grateful if you left a review on Amazon. They help readers decide to give my work a try and I appreciate each one very much.

Thanks again for reading.

Damien Boyd
Devon, UK
February 2014

About the Author

Damien Boyd is a solicitor by training and draws on his extensive experience of criminal law, along with a spell in the Crown Prosecution Service, to write fast paced crime thrillers featuring Detective Inspector Nick Dixon.

Made in the USA
Monee, IL
15 January 2020

20383065R00099